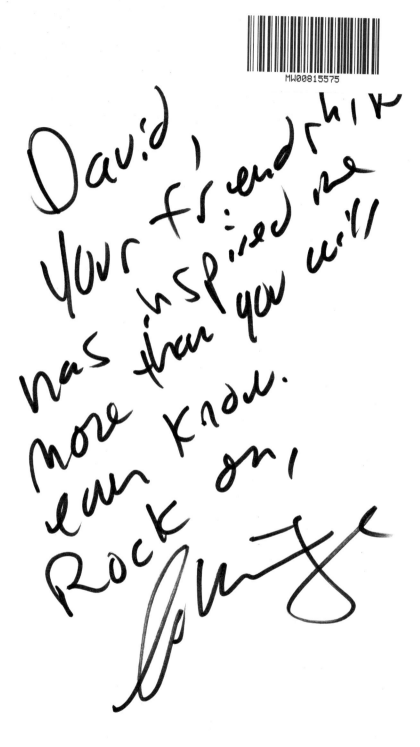

David,
Your friendship
has inspired me
more than you will
ever know.
Rock on,

BACKSLIDE

A novel by

Carl W. Kenney II

Order this book online at www.trafford.com
or email orders@trafford.com

Most Trafford titles are also available at major online book retailers.

This is a work of fiction. All of the characters, names, incidents, organizations, and dialogue
in this novel are either the products of the author's imagination or are used fictitiously.

Printed in the United States of America.

ISBN: 978-1-4269-4149-8 (sc)
ISBN: 978-1-4269-4150-4 (hc)

Library of Congress Control Number: 2010912712

*Our mission is to efficiently provide the world's finest, most comprehensive book publishing
service, enabling every author to experience success. To find out how to publish your
book, your way, and have it available worldwide, visit us online at www.trafford.com*

Trafford rev. 8/25/2010

 www.trafford.com

North America & international
toll-free: 1 888 232 4444 (USA & Canada)
phone: 250 383 6864 ♦ fax: 812 355 4082

WEST AFRICAN
WISDOM

Adinkra Symbols

The symbols used at the beginning of each chapter and to separate sections are West African wisdom symbols. They are used to reflect the diverse spirituality of the author who, in addition to these symbols, uses meaningful quotes at the beginning of each chapter to generate thought related to matters presented in the book. These quotes reflect a variety of theological and philosophical perspectives and divulge the mind of one committed to a celebration of diverse views.

Also by Carl W. Kenney II

Preacha'Man

Dedicated to the loves of my life: my children, Connie Pope and Compassion Ministries of Durham. This is our story.

IMAGINE

-Carl W. Kenney II-

Imagine a world void of the pain caused by some past indiscretion. No memory of the sadness that helped secure this wall of protection. No bittersweet moments. No guilt-filled tears left to soak the humiliation away.

Imagine a time not limited by the mount of fears there to prevent the next step. One more step waiting to explore. One more hope left to wither because it's just too high to climb.

Imagine a dream not deferred by the heat of demon-possessed words and cruel actions. The sting of personal attack can't stop the imagination. The intent of others cannot hinder contemplation.

Imagine a love not subtracted by the addition of some thought not spoken. The fear of judgment doesn't get in the way of the purity of affection. The need for protection is replaced with the joy of inclusion.

My thirst to embrace what is in my imagination has led me to you. You are my last chance to escape my self-destructive ways. You are my last breath before the new day.

You are the beginning of new life. My steps have led me to you. My old dance has changed into a holy two-step.

You are my imagination

JANUARY
Cooperation • Freedom• Change

Do you not know that there comes a midnight hour when everyone has to throw off his mask? Do you believe that life will always let itself be mocked? Do you think you can slip away a little before midnight in order to avoid this? Or are you not terrified by it? I have seen men in real life who so long deceived others that at last their true nature could not Reveal itself ... In every man there is something which to a certain degree prevents him from becoming perfectly transparent to himself; and this may be the case in so high a degree, he may be so inexplicably woven into relationships of life which extend far beyond himself that he almost cannot reveal himself. But he who cannot reveal himself cannot love, and he who cannot love is the most unhappy man of all.

-Soren Kierkegaard-

A RAY OF LIGHT RESTED AT THE FOOT of Simon's bed. His gaze at the beam reminded him of words he had shared before the members of the Shady Grove Baptist Church. Fourteen months had passed since he walked out the back door of the church to capture the love of his life.

The light of hope, the ray of promise, that reminder of God's provision, was there, at the foot of the bed, as he held Jamaica in his arms. The ghost of hurtful moments clouded his imagination while the words of grateful parishioners left a void in his delicate spirit. Simon missed the work of the church.

His prayers seemed feeble as he begged God to take away the thirst for ministry. His work at the university was not enough. "God, show me this too is ministry," he prayed in silence as Jamaica held him tighter. His love for her was not enough to diminish the desire for ministry. He closed his eyes to fight back the tears.

"Why this, Lord?" he prayed as the emotions of his plea brewed within his aching bones. Like that fire shut up in the bones the Prophet Jeremiah wrote about, Simon's drive for service would not go away. "Why this, Lord?" his prayer seemed more like a death wish.

The ray was still there. "What does it mean?" he wondered as he concentrated on its attraction. It was there waiting for him when he opened his eyes. There to force him to contemplate the decision he had made – Jamaica's love over God's call. There after making love. There after saying "I love you, I need you, I'm so thankful you are in my life". The light would not leave him alone.

"Go away and let me rest," he whispered to the light as if the Spirit was waiting to speak to him, reminiscent of the burning bush that swayed Moses to confront a mighty pharaoh. "Let me find my peace. I have served you well. Please leave me alone."

"Good morning baby," Jamaica's moan shattered the silence of his epiphany. "How long you been up?"

"About 30 minutes."

"Um, you have a busy day"

"Yeah, I have a faculty meeting at 9:00 and a class this afternoon."

"Can you meet me for lunch?" she chuckled as she forced her way on top of him. Lunch was their code for sex in the middle of the day.

"I always have time for lunch," he kissed her in that special way. "But before we do lunch can I have some breakfast?"

"You know they say breakfast is the most important meal of the day," she laughed as she kissed his chest while making her way to his stomach and then to where his stiff penis was waiting for her kiss.

They could never get enough of each other. Each knew how to satisfy the other, and their days were filled with thoughts of how the moment of lovemaking would begin. Each loved the touch of the other. Each loved the taste of pleasing the other. Each felt the trembling of love throbbing with every breath.

After savoring each other, after saying I love you over and over again – Jamaica placed his hard penis inside her waiting vagina. The intensity of their foreplay heightened each orgasm she had. Over and over and over again, she came as he held back long enough to satisfy her yearning for pleasure.

"Nobody can do me like you do," she screamed as they climaxed together. "That's the way I like it. That's the way I like it."

They screamed in unison as they ended another installment to prove their love. They rested in each other's arms as the afterglow reminded Simon of why he walked away. The beam was gone now. The only sound was the beat of Jamaica's heart as he placed his head against her breast.

"You sure you have time for lunch," Jamaica chuckled.

"Like I said woman, I always have time for lunch with you."

"Too bad I have to go to work 'cause I would stay here all day and rock your world."

"I know," Simon responded as he thought of his life with Jamaica since leaving Durham, North Carolina to move to Dallas, Texas. Suddenly, the thought of the glaring beam at the foot of the bed vanished long enough for him to relish this mountaintop encounter.

It wouldn't last long. The image of the steady ray revisited his attention as soon as the soothing heat of the water from the shower hit his body. The burst of emotions that inflated his thoughts returned as soon as Jamaica left his side to dry her body. There her voice and touch were not present to take the urge of the call away.

It always came back. No matter how hard he prayed and tried to make it go away, there was a power beyond his own beckoning him to go back to that pain-filled place. That place where insensitivity and misperceptions fueled the opinions of others. Back to that place where mean-spirited people came in sheep's clothing with vicious attacks on the fortitude of men like Simon.

The voice within him would not go away. He stayed there, in the shower, praying the waters would cleanse his desire to go back. He closed his eyes begging for the face of Jamaica to supplant the vision of light. It didn't work. His love was not strong enough to detach him from the passion that called him to serve. Too many hurting people lurking in the shadows of faith needed his strength. His words of inclusion stood as stark contrast to the superficial theology consuming the soul of the Church.

The struggles of the Preacha' Man continued. After walking away for love, he was forced to contend with the consequences of avoiding the call on his life. As much as he wanted to find peace with his new existence, he couldn't. The call would not let him rest. The faces of too many hurting people gripped his soul and drew him back – back to the struggles of ministry.

What would he say to Jamaica?

"Good afternoon Dr. Edwards," one of the students greeted Simon as he walked into his Introduction to Theology class.

"How is everyone today?" he answered as his students prepared to take notes. "I hope all of you found time to enjoy life in the midst of all the work I gave you over the weekend."

"Whatever Dr. Edwards," a student responded. "You treat us like we're grad students."

"That's not true. If you were grad students I would have given you twice the work you received," he snapped back. "I give you so much work because I believe you can handle it. I base what you get from what I believe you can take. To those whom much is given, much is required. Besides, the world needs for you to pave the way to change. Can I get a witness this afternoon?"

"Amen Church," the class responded in harmony. Simon had taught the class to respond to his teaching in the traditional call and response idiom of the black Church. It was his way of making his class fun and to connect him to what he was missing.

"Who has a power quote today from your reading assignment?"

"I do," Bruce jumped up. Students received credit for bringing a quote to class from the reading. The quote became the subject of conversation for the class.

"Preach on my brother," Simon said.

"Grace strikes us when we are in great pain and restlessness," Bruce quoted from Paul Tillich's book Courage to Be. "It strikes us when we walk through the dark valley of a meaningless and empty life. It strikes us when we feel that our separation is deeper than usual, because we have."

"Well done young scholar, tell us why you have selected this quote for today's worship experience."

"Because Tillich focused on the need for self-affirmation despite the threat of non-being," the student responded. "He talks a lot about dread, or anxiety. We need this today in worship because so many of us are anxious about our grade in this class and it's messing with our self-esteem."

"As you should," Simon laughed. "I expect each of you to perform at the level you are capable. No playing in this class. Can the Church say Amen?"

"Amen," the laughter filled the air.

"Tillich spoke of the 'God above God,'" Simon continued. "This is the God that transcends theism. This is the source of our being, the essential being of reason. This is our divine center of wisdom, the human center that is above our understanding. Beyond what we have been taught. Beyond what we feel. This is the God we find when the God we're taught about no longer makes sense."

Simon could tell by the looks on their faces they were grasping the concept. "When all else fails, when the God you're taught about in church no longer makes sense and you find yourself grappling with the assumptions of your faith, there is a God beyond the God of understanding," he continued.

Tillich's *Courage to Be* had carried Simon since leaving the Shady Grove Baptist Church. He often wondered if he had made a mistake by walking away too soon. He missed the emotional burst that came with each Sunday morning celebration. He craved the hum of the Hammond B-3 organ and the lash of the snare drum that paced the clapping of the choir. He missed the shouts and dances of those filled with spirit after a week of toil.

He missed preaching. The words flowed like poetry. He missed people rising on their feet in tribute to getting the message. He missed the tears that couldn't be held back from grown men touched by the words of his message. The smiles, the laughter, the change shared in testimony. Simon missed the Church, and the work of the classroom would never replace the thrill locked in his soul.

He remembered his seven day grapple in deciding if staying was worth all the lies told and the constant attack on his character. They claimed he was gay after he fought for the inclusion of gays and lesbians. They attacked his desire to reach out in support of those addicted to alcohol and other drugs. He fought for the homeless. He fought for the incarcerated. The constant battle to move the people beyond the worship of old time religion drove him away. Despite all the battles he missed the work of the Church.

He missed watching people grow. These students would come for a season – a semester of a year or two – and move to other places. He wasn't able to observe the impact of his teaching. He wouldn't marry them, counsel them, baptize them and watch them share in the work of the kingdom. He would not meet their families and share in each glad moment. They came to be taught, and at the end of the term their joy was in a grade. The defeat was in the same.

Simon needed more than a place to teach – he needed the family back. His time away from ministry had taught him that lesson. The Church is much more than a place to celebrate in worship. It is a home – a gathering of family. He loved the family. He loved its dysfunction. He loved it for what it represented, both good and bad.

His love was deeper than the games played by the people at Shady Grove. He could not forget how deeply scarred he was by their ways. He continued to carry the baggage of his journey. He still cried when he considered how much they hated him, even when he did his best to show the way. He fought back the rage caused by every false rumor and every mean-spirited word launched to tarnish his spirit. He could not deny the anguish caused by living and working among God's people.

Simon fought back the hatred. He learned to love them despite it all. He could because of his Christology. Loving became his ethic. Time had mended the burden of his experience, and now he was prepared to go back. He would not be the same. He could never do it the same and he would not do things for the same reasons as before. He wanted to go back. He wondered how one goes back to revisit pain when the fear found in those memories is still unknown.

"Don't forget, final papers are due next week," Simon concluded class. "I expect masterpieces from each of you."

A few stayed behind to ask questions. There was no gathering at the soul food restaurant to fellowship after the benediction. They went separate ways, to class, back to the dorm, the library. They went to do what students do – prepare to pass each class. They weren't family. They were not enrolled to make life-changing decisions. Simon wanted to believe that his class was making a difference in the formation of their faith, but he knew it would never be the same as in the Church.

He walked to his office, closed the door and prayed. There, in his office, surrounded by the words of Augustine, Barth, Cone, Calvin, Luther, Feuerbach, Gutierrez, Kierkegaard, McFague, Moltmann and others – he prayed. He prayed in a grave of words. "I did not get a PhD to teach, Lord. I did it to preach for you."

His prayer surprised him. It came without warning. "I did not get a PhD to teach, Lord. I did it to preach for you." He had spent the past year attempting to convince himself that teaching was his new calling. He did his best to feel good about walking away from the Church. He wanted to believe that love for Jamaica was worth the sacrifice.

"God give an answer," he prayed. "What does all of this mean?" *Concept of Anxiety*, one of Soren Kierkegaard's books, was on his desk. He nodded in disbelief. He loved the work of the Danish philosopher, theologian and psychologist called the Father of Existentialism.

"God, is Jamaica my Regine?" he prayed. "Am I doomed to make Kierkegaard's mistake?" Regine Olsen was the love of Kierkegaard's life. He proposed to her; however, he soon felt disillusionment and depression about the marriage. Less than a year after he had proposed, he broke it off on August 11, 1841. He wrote in his journal that his 'melancholy' made him unstable for marriage. It's not known why he called off the marriage, but it is clear the two were deeply in love, even after she married Johan Frederik Schlegel. Years later, Kierkegaard asked Regine's husband for permission to speak with her, but he refused. Soon afterwards, the couple left the country after Schlegel was appointed governor in the Danish West Indies. By the time Regine returned, Kierkegaard was dead. She was buried next to him.

Simon believed Kierkegaard maintained that his love for Regine compromised his love for God. His work was impacted by this loss. He regretted his sacrifice to the grave. "Is Jamaica my Regine?" he cried. "Will I miss out on true love because of my love for the work you have given? Will I die like Kierkegaard, hurting because of the ache caused by failing to be with my Regine?"

"Pastor, we really miss you in Durham," Calvin Jenkins, one of the former members at Shady Grove said. The phone call shocked Simon. It was hard to hold back the emotions.

"I think of Shady Grove every day, Calvin. How is the work at the Church?"

"A lot of people left when you walked away. They called an older minister not interested in the kind of work you did. It's just not the same anymore, Pastor."

"That's to be expected Calvin. Each person in ministry has a different calling. It would be a mistake to try to make a person into another me."

"I know Pastor, but man we miss what used to be. It's hard going back to that type of ministry. We miss the teaching. We miss the fun we used to have."

"It's good to know I'm missed Calvin, but people need to find a way to move on without me."

"That's too bad. I've been charged to convince you to come back to Durham," there was a silence.

"You've been charged to do what?"

"To convince you to come back to Durham, Pastor. There's a group of us who want you to come back. We've been meeting on our own, holding Bible Studies and talking about the things you taught us. We tried to stay at Shady Grove, but we just couldn't do it. Not after how things went down."

"It wasn't all that bad Calvin. It's what I needed."

"It was bad, Pastor. The way people falsely accused you. The way Janet did you, having a relationship with one of the members, and people blaming you for her cheating. The way your secretary betrayed you. It was bad, Pastor."

"I survived it Calvin. I learned a lot because of it all."

"We learned a lot too. We learned that we can't be members of a church that treats a person like that. I can't go back and pretend that I'm okay with what those lying devils did to you. I'm angry at what they did to you, but I'm also hurt by what they did to those who needed what you offered."

"I never thought of it that way. I suppose I should have stayed."

"No, you did the right thing. No one believes you should have stayed. You did what you had to do for you, to get away from a work that was beating at your own spirit. We look at it like this time away was your mountaintop experience – a time to rekindle."

"That's true, Calvin. I did need time away."

"Now, it's time to come back home. We need you to come back and finish the work you started."

"I have a new life, Calvin. It's not that easy."

"I know. I know. But can you consider it? Like I said, we been meeting and we are ready to start with a new church. We have 100 people ready to get things going, and there are others ready to join in once they know you coming back."

"That's touching. No one else can take on this role? None of my former ministers come to mind to start the church?"

"That's not up for discussion until you tell us no. Are you telling us no?"

"I need to think and pray over this. I must admit that I have been missing the work of the church. It's not the same. Something is missing with me being a professor."

"So what's the problem?"

"I'm in love."

"I heard about that. It just seems like if she loves you and respects your work she will come with you."

"She has a great job here with the TV station."

"We have TV stations in Durham."

"You make it sound so easy."

"It is if God is in it. Isn't that what you taught us?"

"I know"

"I can do all things through Christ which strengthens me. That's what you taught us Pastor."

"Sounds like you were taking notes."

"Your words and teachings helped change my life. You know that. I've been thirsty for that message since you left. We want you to be happy, Pastor. We want to be family for you. I believe you are supposed to be here, with us, helping us to do the things you taught us before without all that stuff that kept it from happening."

"I have to discuss it with Jamaica."

'That's funny."

"What's funny?"

"When you walked out of the church that day you said you were headed to Jamaica. Everyone thought you were going on a trip. You were talking about her."

"Yeah. I was."

"We don't care about that. That's your business. Janet left to go to Chicago with the stripper. Who can blame you? It must have been hard for you to deal with all of that stuff. Don't know if I could have done it. I respect you for the way you handled it."

"I appreciate that."

"So, did you do it because of her? Is that why you left?"

"I had to decide between my love for myself and her versus my love for Shady Grove. It had a lot to do with her, Calvin, but I had lost a part of myself. I needed to get away from the work because of the way it was changing me. I was doing the work for the wrong reason."

"I get that. What has changed?"

"I have, Calvin. I do want to get back into the church, but I'm not sure what that will look like. I've changed so much and it may mean that you will get something different than what used to be at Shady Grove. Too much has happened and I refuse to go back to being that man."

"Like I said, I understand."

"Your group should pray about that. I need to be sure you're ready to embrace me for the new me. Problem is I can't tell you what that looks like yet. I'm not sure what will be with me because a year has passed. I have to be honest, Calvin, this scares me," there was another pause. Tears were flowing now. Was this Simon's burning bush moment, or was it his temptation in the wilderness.

"We have your back Pastor. Things will be different."

"I want to believe you, Calvin. I need to pray. I'll call you back to let you know," his voice quivered with deep pauses in between each word.

"You okay, Pastor?"

"I will be. It's in God's hands."

"You know we love you, Pastor. We vow not to hurt you."

The meaning of the light came to him. It was there to prepare him, to warn him, to guide him in this moment. This was his road less traveled. Again, he stood in a moment of decision. Before, it was the burden of love in battle with the call of the kingdom. Love and peace of mind won that fierce combat. Before, it was the agony of rejection in collision with his need for serenity. He grappled with his need to be liberated from a painful marriage – two of them. His union with Janet had died years before the eulogy. His marriage with the church was mired by the onslaught of personal attacks.

Before, he needed to be set free. His walk down the middle aisle to exit the door of the church freed him of years of frustration. Instead of coming in, down the middle aisle, he walked out, down the middle aisle – away from marriages to his partners –the church and his wife. Away from the words of attack and the depression stirred by regret. He was free now. Free to love and embrace the better things in life. He loved his freedom. No glares from the crowd. No words of rebuke or stabs in his back to keep him tiptoeing through life in anticipation of yet another disappointment.

Finally, he was free. Free to love and experience life. Free to breathe again but the call would not let him rest, and the light would not leave him. It followed him, reminding him that life for him is that road less traveled. The burn of the bush, the small still voice, the echo of the ages reminded him of his purpose. He walked away for a season, but he could not walk away.

Simon placed the plate on a romantically decorated table. Candle lights flickered, setting the mood as Miles Davis' horn sprayed the room with an aura that reminded Jamaica of their first kiss. The meal: Moroccan-Style Braised Chicken Thighs with Preserved Lemons and Green Olives. For dessert: Chocolate-Hazelnut Tart.

Simon had taken his time to establish an ambiance befitting of their love. What they shared was the stuff written about in romance novels. Being together felt like an endless orgasm with goose bumps, curled toes and rapid beating hearts to accent each breath taken. Their love and their being together were conceived after years of separation. After years of wondering and regret, she appeared again. There wasn't enough time to make up for the wasted memories – the ones that could have been theirs if not for the tragedy of timing.

"Damn baby," Jamaica screeched with unbridled anticipation. "You must really want the pussy tonight. Mama gonna take care of you for this!"

They laughed as always knowing that making love was something they both wanted. Something they both needed to express what their vocabularies were incapable of uttering. Simon wasn't so sure it would end that way. The news he had to share was certain to pour chilly water on their passion.

"Baby, you know I love cooking for you. You can thank Emeril for tonight's dish."

"Fuck Emeril! I want the chef to get between my legs."

He sat next to her and gently touched her thigh with his index finger. "Don't start nothing you can't finish, Rev," she joked. That word chilled his mood – Rev. Another reminder of the decision he had to make. Another word among the countless others – preacher, church, God, Jesus, Amen – to force recollections of his former life as the Preacha' Man. He closed his eyes to constrain the thought. As Jamaica sucked the bone of a chicken thigh, he focused on her thigh.

"You just have to distract me don't you," she moaned as he made his way to the floor where he kneeled between her legs.

"Just eat baby. Just eat. Let me take care of you while you eat."

He kissed her thigh, hoping, praying that it would be enough to take the thought away – Rev. "I love you so much," his voice trembled as he opened her legs and kissed her inner thigh. First the left, then the right. "I love you so much it hurts."

As Jamaica enjoyed the dish on the table, Simon enjoyed the dish under the table. He knew that it might be his last supper. Things would never be the same after he shared the news of the day. How could he live void of this love? – He thought as his lips kissed her dripping love.

He could never get enough of her taste. His rapid descent to her thighs could not be defied. He could not stop himself. His love would not let him stop. For years his body ached for a way to be free from the oppressive ways of black faith. For far too long he denied himself the satisfaction of embracing love in the way he did with Jamaica. Authentic love, according to traditional faith claims, could only be expressed within the context of marriage.

For too long, he hated his sexuality. He prayed for urges to go away. They never did. He lived quenching his thirst for a satisfying sex life. He did not have it in his marriage. He prayed hard to fight the desire to be with other women, to cheat on his wife to gratify his natural cravings.

The sobs became intensified with each kiss. There, under the table, away from the stare of Jamaica, he shed tears. He baptized her thighs with his tears. He would miss her touch. He would crave her love, and he knew it would never go away. He would ache for her body like a crack addict craving another hit. She provided that sacred touch that sanctified his emotions. She balanced his life like the Holy Ghost on Pentecost. Agony and frustration had no place while he settled in her arms. He felt the victory that brought meaning to scripture – 'I can do all things through Christ which strengthens me.'

Jamaica was the missing rib that God placed in his side to bring comfort to a once miserable life. Jamaica was his helpmate, his leaning cane in time of trouble. She was the bright colors used by God to paint breathtaking landscapes for the two of them to admire. Their life together was a masterpiece created by God. Their hearts beat in unison. Their footsteps seemed ordered by higher powers. Their words were laced with visions of better days. Their days were filled with thoughts of the next kiss – waiting, hoping for another chance to say I love you.

This is that rare love conceived in movies. This is that unique embrace many concede will never be. It comes around only once in a lifetime, and, when it does, it is best to never, ever let it go – he could hear the voice of wisdom challenging him with each kiss not to walk away from this love.

She was his Isaac held before God as the sacrifice to prove his dedication. He waited for his ram in the bush. He kissed Jamaica's thighs, now soaked with his tears, and prayed one last time. "Please God, don't make me walk away from this," he moaned now trembling from the silence. "Please, don't make me sacrifice this love."

He felt crazy for having to let it go. For the first time he understood what it meant to be called to this work. Simon reflected on his ordination. They asked him then about his calling. The ordination council asked him how he knew he was called. He gave a lame answer about hearing God's voice. He believed each word then. He believed it was his dreams and visions coupled with the voice of God that called him to this work. He could not deny that calling, but his urge to be free – to love without restraint – made it hard to say yes to God's will.

"Baby, you okay down there," Jamaica moaned after releasing her passion. Simon locked his arms around her warm thighs, resting his head in her lap like a pillow wrapped in silk.

"I love you so much," he answered. "I don't want to let you go."

"Then don't," her reply seemed so easy. The silence said it all. She waited, unwearyingly for a patented Simon comeback. He held her, sobbing as if death had come to take her away. He held her, like the last word before the last goodbye.

She pulled back her chair, and reached down. "Come here baby. Come here and hold me."

He rose from the floor, lifted her out of the chair and sat where she had been. She cuddled in his arms, kissing the tears away. "What's wrong, baby? I can tell something is wrong."

Where do you begin, he thought as she opened the door for the conversation that was waiting to be had. How do you tell the woman you love that love may not be enough? "It's all so confusing," he whispered.

"What did you say baby?"

"I said it is all so confusing."

"What's confusing?"

"My call," that word set the stage-call. For some, it was God talk used to inspire people to give to the work of the kingdom. Those pulpit pimps used it, manipulated the people, by using that word – call – to set them apart from the rest. It implied the hearing of a strange voice outfitted with a challenge to give up, to walk away for the sake of a higher purpose.

Jamaica's abhorrence of that word was the one source of conflict that mired their love. She couldn't understand the concept of being pushed by God to do a work. She refused to accept that God would force a person to sacrifice a good thing for a divine purpose. Jamaica believed in a person's freedom to live in the way they wish void of divine intrusion.

The moment was mired by that word. "I thought we had moved past that," Jamaica exhaled as her arms loosened in response to what she felt coming.

"I'm sorry baby. It won't go away."

"What won't go away?"

"I miss the church."

"I thought your work at the university took care of that," she said while moving to the couch on the other side of the room.

"It's not the same," he wished it were the same.

"So, what am I supposed to do with that?"

"I can't tell you what to do. I only know what I wish for us."

"What? That I be the damn first lady of some fucking church?"

"I know that's not you baby."

"Yeah, you knew that when you decided to come down here to be with me. You told me you were ready to start a new life away from the church. How am I supposed to take it when you tell me you are feeling a damn call to go back to all of that?"

"It's hard to explain."

"It sure is. How do you explain wanting to go back to that shit? Those motherfuckers took all of your goodness and stepped on it like you was a piece of shit. They talked about you and then smiled in your fucking face, and you want me to understand being called to go back to that," she stood with hands on hips in a tone that demanded his attention.

"It's God who …"

"To Hell with that shit! You telling me that God would want you to be treated like that! You must think you're fucking Jesus. What kind of damn God do you serve to take all of that?"

"All I can say is I'm called to help people," he took a few steps in her direction.

"Let them help their damn self. Shit why can't God just let us take care of each other without all of that shit that comes with your fucking call," her changed mood refused to accept the offer of his approach.

"This is what I have given my life to, baby. This is what I'm trained to do."

"You have a fucking Ph.D.," her frustration was swelling. "Aren't you trained to use that degree to teach? Why can't you just be happy with using that fine mind of yours without all the shit that comes with dealing with ungrateful Niggers?"

"I can't help you see it baby. I wish I could," he felt the disappointment of his own words.

"So, what does all of this mean for me, huh? What does it mean for me," the quiver in her voice served as the prelude to what would follow.

Simon paused to get the courage to say it. Was he sure he wanted to say it? Could he, should he take the risk of saying it, knowing that once said he could never turn back? "I got a call from Durham on yesterday," his mumbled words vibrated in his head.

"Uh ha, a call from who? Who in the fuck called you from Durham?"

"Calvin."

"Who the fuck is Calvin? Some motherfucker from that damn church?"

"He was a member at Shady Grove"

"What, he call to tell you they miss your black ass? How many times I have to hear that," she moved to a chair on the other side of the room, creating as much distance as she could from the pain of his words.

"Don't be mad, baby," he took the risk by taking two steps in her direction.

"I'm not mad. I'm frustrated because of how it seems like I will spend the rest of my life being the one who comes between your fucking work. I don't understand it, but you just won't let it go and be at peace. So, what Calvin talking about?"

"They want me to come back to Durham to start a new church," the words shifted the mood to yet another level. He stood over her now.

"They want you to do what!"

"To start a new church," her tear packed eyes frowned at the proclamation.

"Damn, don't we have enough fucking churches in the world without starting a new one? Are you telling me you want to go back to Durham?"

"I'm telling you I don't feel like I have a choice."

"You right, I'll never understand that shit. We always have a choice. So, you telling me you want to go back to Durham. You want to walk away from everything we have built together over the past year to go back," she stood close enough for him to feel the heat of her breath.

"I was hoping you would understand."

"I understand that your black ass is crazy if you think I understand why you would walk away from a great job, home and what we have to be hurt again," her swagger suggested a pride too strong to accept his truth. She strolled in circles in search of words to defeat his claim.

"It is crazy. I know it's crazy," Jamaica's words made perfect sense. Simon found it difficult to believe what he was saying. He wondered if he had lost his mind. "I'm crazy to think about leaving all of this. Why don't you come with me?"

"Why won't I come with you! Why would I walk away from an anchor gig in a top twenty market? Huh? Why would I sacrifice what I have worked all of my life for to go backwards? Do you think I'm crazy too?"

"No, I thought you loved me enough to make that sacrifice for me."

"Oh, so now it's payback season. Fuck that. Just because you walked away to come down here I'm supposed to do the same for you? Is that what you think," her voice found keys on the anger scale never heard before. The sound vibrated against the walls and kept beating against Simon's fragile self-esteem.

"I hoped you would see it that way."

"I bet you would. One problem. I never asked you to come down here. I was happy with the way things were. You came on your own. No pressure from me. If I was okay without you then, why would I give up my dream now?"

"I was hoping it had something to do with your loving me more now," Simon followed her around the room as she refused to look at him.

"That's bullshit Simon. Of course I love you more now. We've gotten to know each other better over the past year. Yes, I want to spend the rest of my life with you, but I'm not giving up my life to spend my life with you," she stopped her prance to nowhere and poked her fist in his chest.

"I get it, it's okay for me to sacrifice my life, but you can't do that for me. Is that it? All that matters is what you get out of it. Imagine your life without your work. Think about how you would feel if you went to teach journalism at a university. Would you be happy with not being on TV every night," his words served as payback.

"The difference is they don't force me into being something I'm not. I'm free to be myself."

"That's bullshit, Jamaica. You have to be what they want too. You have to look the way they want you to look. You have to talk the way they want you to talk. When you don't they will kick your ass out as soon as the numbers don't line up. Your work is no different than what I do. The only difference between me and you is you buy into the image they have of you. You play that fucking game, smiling at motherfuckers when you're out in public. Dressing the way they want you to dress. You have sold out to them as much as I have to give up part of myself for the church," Simon didn't want this, but his true emotions were beginning to come to the surface.

"Don't make this about me, Simon. This is about your weak ass," they stood face to face now with their emotional weaponry pulled in wait of the next shot taken.

"Oh, I'm weak because I understand my purpose? No, I'm crazy because I have a love for the work of the church. Is that what makes me crazy, Jamaica? What I do is no different than anyone else. Yes, I'm called to this work, just like you are called to take the shit that comes with sitting in front of that camera every night to present that fake-ass façade."

"I'm not fake!"

"You're not? What would your viewers of the Bible belt think if they knew you have problems with the faith they profess? Would your numbers drop? What would those fine Christians think if they knew you lived with a former pastor and that you are a bona fide freak who fucked him when he was still married? Would they call the station to complain if they knew the truth about you? The only reason you still have your fucking job is because they haven't caught wind of the real you. Why? Because you live this fake life. I have no problem with doing what you need to do to survive, but don't criticize my work and calling because I was man enough to be honest with the people. I took that risk because I wanted to be real. You love that cash money too much for that"

"If you feel that way, why you still here?"

"Because I do love you. Because I want you in my life. Yes, I loved you enough to move to be with you. I hoped you would be willing to do the same for me, but now I see you love your life without me more than you love me," his tears matched hers now. The agony of the years flooded the room.

"That's cold."

"Is it? What you have said is cold. You criticize my faith. You question my mental stability. All of this is about me fitting into your world, Jamaica. I'm willing to do that, but when do you prove to me that you are willing to fit into my world? Huh, are you willing to give just a little to hold onto what we have or am I just a piece of furniture to be moved when you desire?"

"Don't be blaming me for your being here. You made that decision on your own,"

"You don't get it! I have no regrets. I did the right thing in coming to be with you. I loved you enough to make that decision. Loving you set me free from where I was. I'm free to do things different now, Jamaica. I have learned deep lessons about me. I took that risk and I'm better for it, but it would be nice, just once, if someone would make sacrifices for me in the way I have."

"That's your shit, Simon. You can't expect me to be you."

"You're right, but you can't expect me to be you. I am a pastor. That's my call. That's my fucking passion. As much as you hate what I do, it's what I do, and I need you to support me in that rather than trying to make it all fit into a world that makes you feel better."

"Does this mean you're going?"

"It means I have no choice but to go. I wanted to make life right with you, but being here forced me to deny a part of myself to be with you. I need to be speaking hope into the lives of those who need me. I can't rest knowing God has given me so much to give back and all I do with it is teach fucking philosophy and theology classes. Yes, I'm good as a teacher, but I'm called to make a difference."

"Okay, okay! I get it. I do understand," Jamaica sat on the couch hoping to fight the tears. She couldn't. It was too much to bear. "I do understand, Simon. This is what I've been scared of. How in the Hell am I supposed to compete with God?"

"You can only be you, Jamaica. You don't understand that part of me. You have never seen me in that role before. You know a side of me. There's another side that I miss. I wish you could be with me in that work," he sat next to her. He wished he could explain the light. He wished the light would allow him to work in a church in Dallas rather than going back to that painful place.

"Yeah right, a fucking first lady with a big hat sitting on the front row, waving a paper fan with Martin Luther King, Jr. on the front."

"One part of that is right. Marry me. Go with me. Support me, baby. Together we can make it work," he took her hand in wait. He waited for yes I will. He waited for of course I will.

"You would like that."

"I would."

"I wish I could, baby. You're the first man I've ever thought about marrying," her eyes said yes, but something was missing.

"Damn, that's a shock."

"It shouldn't be. I do love you," he held her as she cried. Maybe she always knew this day would come, the end of what seemed too good to be true. Too good for until death do us part. Too good for kiss the bride. She wanted Simon in her life, yet being with her denied him a part of himself that would not go away with time. She released him to go back to the den of lions. Back to the valley of dry bones where misery knew him by name.

"I wish you loved me more than that fucking calling," Jamaica screamed. Her words said it all. Why should a person be forced to decide between love and calling? Why leave a comfortable place to seek the unknown?

January, the month of new beginnings. Resolutions unveiled at midnight give reason for hope in a better year. January, the month of change and transition. The month of moving forward while looking back.

Over the next month, Simon planned for change. He looked back, hoping things would be different when he settled on the land of troubled memories. He looked back at a year of love and wondered how he would survive without it. He looked forward to making a difference.

"Not my will, your will be done," he prayed. "Amen."

FEBRUARY

Supremacy of God • Transformation • Leadership

Our language has wisely sensed the two sides of being alone. It has created the word loneliness to express the pain of being alone. And it has created the Word solitude to express the glory of being alone.
-Paul Tillich-

SIMON BOARDED THE PLANE on February 15th- the day after Valentine's Day. The Dallas heat mocked his attempt to remain cool. He packed just enough to get through the week; the movers were set to pick up his things in two days. It all seemed like a dream, or maybe he had awakened from the trance to return to his reality – the work of the church. Back to life in Durham, North Carolina, where skeletons from his past still lurked waiting to pound his confidence.

The last night with Jamaica was a reminder of what could have been. Her soft seductive touch had him contemplating the strength of his decision. Her eyes said stay. The tears made it harder to resist the urge to remain locked in her arms. The light would not let him stay.

One last peek at the ticket – Continental flight 623. He would arrive in Durham at 4:35 p.m. He hadn't been back since he left the city. Leaving was much easier than coming back. There were no regrets. There were no back and forth emotions that had him trapped, scrutinizing the past. When he walked away he left behind the burden of ministry. He left behind an addiction to animated worship. He walked away from carrying people's burdens and hurting when he couldn't take the pain away. Then the light appeared.

That last week in Durham forced him to face his true self. He pondered the things he had hidden from – things too dark and hideous to meet in the day. Things like a ride in a truck that ended with a gag of a forced penis in his mouth when he was too young to understand. He sifted through the weeds of a brutal past that made it difficult to tell the truth – his manhood was violated by a man, and he was afraid to speak that truth.

His truth would cause others to question his manhood. They would assume him gay due to the actions of a mad man. Freedom came in telling the truth, but telling it came with a price – the perceptions of other people. In going back, he would have to tell the truth. He could not function in the same way. His life was adjusted by those dreadful memories. The loss of his innocence tarnished his past, and impacted the way he labored in ministry, but now, he believed, he was free to serve with power.

During that week before leaving, he faced almost getting high again. The fear of relapse catapulted him over the wall he had created to hide his pain. It moved him away from the compulsion to please others, and into the world of truth telling. His truth alienated others. His facade kept him from his true self –a self waiting, begging to come out and play. His world was turned upside down; inside out as he rode a roller coaster headed nowhere. Around and around he went, hoping it would stop. It never did. Monday felt like Tuesday. Tuesday was the same as Wednesday. Each day was the same day.

The collision that pitted his past with his present forced a shift in the way he functioned. He could no longer hide behind the holy garments and sanctified emotions of black faith. He couldn't shout the hurt away. He couldn't find his way to those weekly mountaintop encounters with lofty promises of a better day. He needed resolve from the riddle of his misery. It took action. The only way to make the pain go away was to walk away from the source of it all.

By walking out the back door of the Shady Grove Baptist Church, Simon gave himself permission to live again. He took the cross off his back and forced the Church to carry its own load. He couldn't wipe their tears away. He didn't have the keys to unlock the door of pleasure they sought each week. He was limited. It was time to step away from that lofty place created by those who saw God in him. He said no to their need to worship him.

He said yes to what felt good – Jamaica. He was going back to the pain-filled land of his past, but it would be different this time. He could not do it their way again. He had changed. He walked in his newfound freedom, and Simon was not willing to let it go.

Grabbing his bags, Simon found his seat next to the window. The stress of the departure was getting the best of him. As excited as he was to return to Durham, he would miss teaching. More than anything, he would miss having Jamaica as a companion. For the first time in his life, he had discovered the pleasures that come with having a woman like her in his life. He closed his eyes for one last prayer.

"God, grant me the serenity to accept the things I cannot change, the courage to change the things I can, and the wisdom to know the difference," the serenity prayer had helped him through many hardships. Through his battle with addiction. Through the guilt that came with divorce. Through the pain that came from walking away from work he loved. Now, he needed serenity. He took a deep breath, reached inside his bag and pulled out Don Miquel Ruiz's book *The Four Agreements.* The book helped him center his spirit. Those four simple agreements: be impeccable with your words, don't take anything personally, don't make assumptions, and always do your best – helped him remain focused.

The seat next to his was empty as the stewardess gave instructions before takeoff. A distinguished man sat in the aisle seat. His silver hair made it difficult to deduce his age. His dark tan gave the impression that he had spent time away in some exotic place. It was February, and the chill of winter had sucked the flush from the faces of most Caucasians across America. Simon wondered if he lived in Dallas, or if he lived and worked in Durham. He placed a stack of papers in the empty seat. "Do you mind," he asked Simon.

"Go for it" Simon murmured as he did his best to squeeze his 6'3" frame into the compact space.

He quickly reviewed the work before the stewardess came to inform him all items had to be placed under the seat in front of him.

He made it just in time. "I hate having to work while traveling," he said while placing his files in the proper place.

"I do understand that," Simon responded. "It's bad enough that we have to get in this thing."

They both laughed.

"I know. I used to have a fear of flights. Couldn't get me in a plane if my life depended on it," the man said.

"My father won't fly," Simon responded. "He had a bad flight back in the late '60s and kissed the ground when he landed. He said he thanked God for getting him through the flight and vowed never to do it again."

"Fear is a terrible thing."

"It certainly is," Simon said while thinking about how fear had limited his life. "How did you get over your fear?"

"I asked God to take it away," the man answered. "I had a chance for a big deal right after finishing my MBA. The company I worked for needed for me to fly to San Francisco to close the deal. I refused to go because I was afraid to fly. I got fired because of my fear. I lost a good job because I wasn't willing to get past my fear."

"That's enough to get you to rethink your fear," Simon chuckled.

"It was my dream job. After graduating from Wharton I had my pick of the litter. I thought I was a stud. I was one of the smartest in my class. I had the gift of gab, you know, I was arrogant like that. I really believed I was on top of the world. I was humbled because of my one fear. One thing came between me and my becoming the success I felt I would always be."

"How did you turn it around?"

"I had to turn it over to God. I lost everything. That's a bad feeling. I went from the big shot to a man reduced to his fears. God humbled me. I gave my life over to Christ. I asked God to take my fears away," the man hesitated. "I had to be broken before I could be elevated."

"That's an amazing story"

"My name is Melvin Webb. I'm the CEO of Telepath in the Research Triangle Park,"

"I've heard about your company. You're doing some great work."

"We try our best to balance things if you know what I mean."

"Say more."

"Well, like anyone in business, I'm about making as much money as I can."

"Nothing wrong with that."

"I like to believe that God places some of us in position to be a blessing in the kingdom. My simple fear of flying kept me from my purpose. God has since given me the courage to move past any fear. I can do all things through Christ."

"I can get with that."

"I'm glad to hear that. So many people in the world of business don't get it. I pray constantly that God will use me to expand the work of the kingdom. I don't know how, but I'm praying for God to show me the way."

"I will be in prayer with you on that."

"I didn't get your name."

"Simon Edwards," the two reached across the chair to shake hands.

"Simon Edwards. Your name sounds familiar. Simon Edwards. Are you Reverend Simon Edwards?"

"Yes."

"It's a small world," Melvin chuckled. "I visited Shady Grove when I was an undergraduate student at Duke. I was the white boy with no rhythm clapping when the choir sang."

"It is a small world. I have a secret for you. Some black folks don't have rhythm." Both exploded in laughter.

"All I can remember is it seemed like I was the only one who didn't have any."

"That's too funny."

"I heard you left the church."

"I did. It was a little over a year ago."

"That had to be tough. I read the story in the Herald-Sun. They gave you a tough time over there. Did it have anything to do with your dreadlocks? I like them."

"The change in me had a lot to do with it. By the way, I call them locs, not dreadlocks. Makes it sound like they are something to be dreaded."

"That's a good point. What changed in you?"

"The way I viewed myself as a servant of the church changed. I locked my hair because I wanted a spiritual overhaul. It forced me to focus on who I am as a person versus what other people saw when they looked at me. It was best for me to leave, Melvin. It was time to go."

"It's so sad that you had to go. The church was making a major impact on so many lives. It had a lot to do with my spiritual development."

"Praise God for that."

"So, what are you doing now?"

"I'm heading back to Durham to start a new church."

"Fantastic! I'm so happy for you."

"I'm walking in faith, Melvin. I had a great life back in Dallas."

"Isn't that what faith is about?"

"Yeah, going somewhere without knowing where you are going."

"That's it."

"I had a great life, Melvin," Simon felt the swell of his emotions. There on a plane, headed back to the valley – the place where pain consumed him – he felt the weight of his decision. "I had a great life."

"Was it work or love?"

"It was love."

"You walked away from love to serve God. That's a big sacrifice, Simon. God honors that form of sacrifice."

"I'm not so sure about that. I do know that it hurt having to stand in the middle of love and God."

"So, you left the church for love, and now you leave love for the church."

"Yeah. Isn't that deep."

"There must be a lesson in it all, Simon."

"I just pray to be faithful, Melvin. I don't want my fears to control me," the word shocked him. Was the purpose of this meeting to discuss his fears? Melvin smiled.

"You can't fly my friend, until you rid yourself of all your fears."

"Is that what all of this is about? My fears?"

"Simon, have you read *The Celestine Prophecy*?"

"I have."

"Then you know from reading that book there are no coincidences in life. All is ordered with a purpose in mind. Each person carries energy that can either add to or draw from those they meet. I'm sensing that my energy is adding to your energy."

"That's true. I suppose there is a reason for our meeting. I wasn't aware that I'm carrying fear with me."

"You know that life is like an onion. That we have so many layers to pain we carry into the work of the kingdom. I would be shocked if you weren't a bit afraid. It takes tremendous courage to go back to what God delivered you from with a faith that it will be different this time."

"All I know is I'm called to do this work. I believe there is unfinished business in Durham."

"And you're probably unclear about what that work will be like."

"That's true."

"Isn't that what faith is all about? I remember how hard it was for me to start my own business. That's why I'm so encouraged by your starting this new ministry. My going into business went against everything I had imagined for my life. Everything I touched turned into gold."

"Is that supposed to encourage me," Simon laughed.

"No, it's to warn you. M. Scott Peck wrote about the road less traveled. Starting something new takes vision. It takes faith. It takes a desire to do things in a way that is unlike anything else. You can't be what you used to be. The problem is you don't know who you are in this new work. It will take time to get a feel for your new wings. When you do, then you can fly."

"It sounds like you should be doing this instead of me."

"It's all the same thing, Simon. The work of a new business and the work of the church are the same when both are understood to be callings from God."

"How long did it take for you to know it would be okay?"

"At the point when I released my desire to do things my way. It took my no longer worrying about traditional measures of success. I had to get rid of my expectations. Simon, I had to stop doing the things I had been trained to do. I began focusing on who I am as a servant of God, and learned to be at peace with myself. That's when things turned around for me."

"It's so much, Melvin. I don't even know where to start."

"Good. Trust your people. God will lead the way. Take care of you. Never forget that your healing is important."

The flight attendant interrupted the conversation with the news the plane would land soon. Melvin promised to be in touch and to pray for Simon. Simon left believing God had sent Melvin to prepare the way – like John the Baptist with Jesus. As he contemplated that possibility, he remembered that Jesus was sent into the wilderness to be tempted by the devil after his baptism.

Was this his blessing or his backslide? Was he going back to the fire to be tortured, or would he come out on the other side refined by the flame? Was he backsliding into bitterness? Was this his punishment for infidelity and for walking away from his children? Was Jamaica his slice of heaven on earth, or the personification of Satan clad in sexy garments?

He stepped off the plane. Too late to turn back now. Only time would tell, but the words of Melvin helped pave the way.

"Pastor!" Carmen was the first to greet Simon as he entered the room. She hugged him while refusing to control her emotions. "It's my Pastor! It's my Pastor!"

Her shout evoked memories of a special bond grounded in things in common. She, like Simon, had overcome her addiction. He met her on the streets near the place where he was tempted to buy drugs after a heated meeting at Shady Grove. "Are you the police?" the dealer asked.

"No, I'm not the police," he thought. "I'm the pastor of the church from around the corner." He pulled away to begin his journey to overcome the pain that almost led him to relapse that night.

Carmen, like Simon, had endured sexual abuse. He remembered the day in the truck when a family friend forced him to suck his dick. He was too young to understand, and too scared to tell his parents.

Their bondage to drugs was fueled by a need to forget the images in their heads when they closed their eyes. He smiled as he remembered when she told him her name – Carmen - the same as his daughter.

Everyone stood and clapped as Carmen allowed her love for Simon to provide the context for the beginning of a new work. Everyone in the room knew the story. Simon found Carmen on the streets. She was an addict and a prostitute who found the courage to tell her story before the members of the Shady Grove Baptist Church. In the process she exposed Deacon Andrews for his hypocrisy. He had sexually abused her when she was much younger, and his cruelty began her cycle of addiction and sexual deviance.

"I'm so glad to see you, Carmen," Simon's emotions overwhelmed him. He had prayed that his leaving Shady Grove would not result in Carmen's relapsing. He had wanted to help her reclaim her life, but couldn't stay. The pain of remaining would not let him stay. He had stayed for others, but, that time, he couldn't stay. He had needed to walk away.

"I'm still clean, Pastor," she hugged him tight. "Look at me! Look at what God has done for me, Pastor. It's because of how God used you that night. I went back to school. I'm working. I have my own place. I feel good about myself for the first time in a long time, and I got my Pastor standing here to let the world know that God can do anything if you trust him with your life. Look at me! Look at me! Look at what God has done."

There wasn't a dry eye in the room. "God is able Carmen," Simon said. His baritone voice stirred the imaginations of the women in the crowd. It was hard to tell if it was their faith in his proclamations or his luring looks and charisma that led them to follow him.

"You are a miracle. It's because of you and people like you that I'm here today. Our work in Durham isn't done. Do you hear me, Carmen? No, does everyone hear me? Our work in Durham isn't done."

Everyone stood and clapped. It was one of those authentic moments that lets people know God is present. There, in a room at the Downtown Durham Public Library, a movement began. There was no building to house the association. No sound system to boost Simon's eloquent words. No choir to draw the masses or plan for social action. No deacons or trustees or ushers or youth volunteers.

Simon took a look at the crowd. Close to 200 people were jammed tight. They had prayed for his return. Steve Cruz was there. Chanti Stephens was there. Mary Collins was there. He smiled as he noticed the faces of those who had stood by his side over the years. Bonita was there. He remembered the rumors about the two of them. Their friendship was misconstrued as a romantic bond.

Simon learned a lesson in confronting the gossip related to Bonita. He had used his friendship to replace something missing in his marriage. Although they never had sex, they never kissed; he wanted to kiss her, he wanted to make love. They had an intimate relationship that combated the bond he had with Janet, his wife. He pretended it was innocent because there was no sex involved, but everything else was present. The love for one another, the desire for more, the intense conversations, and the willingness to sacrifice for the other – it was all there.

He nodded at Bonita. She smiled in a way that released both of them from any anxiety that may have existed before he stepped in the room. He knew this new saga required a safe distance from her, and she knew any thoughts of more would put Simon at risk of being viewed in a way worse than before.

The old swagger was back. He paced the room with a deep confidence that inspired the roar of the amen corner His locs flowed down his back evoking images of the command of Absalom, the son of King David, who died from his dreadlocks tangled in the trees before an arrow pierced his heart.

"Let's talk about how I got here," Simon began. "There was a light. It met me every morning to start my day. There, at the foot of my bed, every day for the past six months, a light appeared. It was for me like Moses' burning bush. It never spoke. It just stared at me, challenging me, chastising me, calling me to come back home."

"Preach, pastor," Steve said.

Simon took off his jacket. "I think I will, Steve," the crowd clapped in anticipation. They had waited to hear Simon preach again. They needed his words to lift their spirits again. "I couldn't hide from the light. I would lie there, in the bed, gaping at that light. I would take my shower and sing my song. You all know my song. I would sing 'I won't complain' to remind me of how blessed I am. You know my song. I would sing 'What a Friend I have in Jesus' to consider the significance of our closeness. You know my song. I would sing 'Lead Me, Guide Me' to prepare myself for another day. Yes, I would sing my song, there in the shower," the crowd felt the passion of his words.

"It would find me there, in the shower. The light would be there gawking at me. It wouldn't let me rest, but followed me from room to room. 'What is it, light? What truth is there in your presence? Are you here to show the way like the cloud of Moses? Are you here to warn me? What is your purpose?' I would speak to the light."

"For six months I asked that question. 'What is your purpose? Have any of you asked that question – what is your purpose, light? Why do you follow me? Why do you haunt my days? What message do you hold from the divine to pave my way? Are you the light unto my path? Show me the way, light, but first, tell me your purpose'."

"I waited for six months. There was no answer, just the light. I prayed. No answer. I waited. No answer. I hoped. No answer. I fasted and prayed. No answer. Just a light, every day, waiting for me."

"Finally it came to me. It took me by surprise. It was that moment of transcendence that awakened my spirit. It forced me to reconsider my comforts, and to place them in the proper place. Sometimes you have to rethink your comforts. My life was at peace. I enjoyed my work. God gave me a chance at love. After years of brokenness and heartbreak, deception and discontentment, failure and facades, I felt free. Let me tell you a secret. Feeling free is not the same as being free. Something was missing. The light was there to help me find my way."

"I was asking the wrong question. You see, I was praying to the light. I assumed it was God's messenger. That was my mistake. The light didn't belong to God, the light belonged to me. My light was outside of me. It was there begging to get back into my life. It was still there, but it was not a part of me. It was there to remind me of my purpose. It was there to challenge my comforts and to point me back to my purpose. It was my light shining."

"You see, I was singing the wrong song. I should have been singing 'This Little Light of Mine, I'm Gonna Let it Shine'. I should have been singing that. God placed the light there to remind me that I am the light of the world. My light was hidden somewhere reserved for those afraid to shine."

"I had to take my light back. I had to let it shine again. Oh, but there's good news today. God wouldn't let my light go away. It followed me through the day. It woke me up every morning. It wouldn't let me get away. God is like that. She shows your true self when you do all you can to walk away. She forces you to come back to your light – to find your true essence – and be that light for others to see."

"That's why I'm back. I'm here to be light again. To shine before men and women, boys and girls, black and white, Hispanic and Asians who are looking for another way. I'm here to love my gay and lesbian brothers and sisters. They need light too. There will be no hatred here. There will be no backbiting and gossip-filled conversations here. There will be no heated meetings loaded with hatred. There will be no pity parties or angry walks back down memory lane.

"We have to be, we must be the light of the world. Do you hear me, Carmen? God needs your light. God needs all of our lights to shine, and we can't waste energy in watching our light remain detached from our spirits. That's your light waiting on you to catch up with the real you. That's your light challenging you to be the real you."

The light filled the room. A representative from the library stepped into the room to inform the group they were making too much noise. It was too late. They were standing and singing together. "This little light of mine, I'm gonna let it shine. This little light of mine, I'm gonna let it shine. This little light of mine, I'm gonna let it shine. Let it shine, let it shine, let it shine." The public library became holy ground. The light of hope illuminated sacred space as the group began a new journey. It was a Tuesday evening. Sunday was around the corner. There was no home to house those in the room, but faith would carry them to their Promised Land. They trusted God, and Simon was home to help them see the way.

There were no classes in divinity school to prepare Simon for starting a new church. So much of what it takes to be a vital ministry can be taken for granted. For the next three days Simon, Calvin, Steve and Chanti worked to pull things together for worship on Sunday. They needed a place to meet. They needed to provide for music. They needed to get the word out.

Simon contacted Matthew Drake about being the minister of music. He had played organ at Shady Grove, and Simon was impressed with his talent. He was part of a group called Durti Sol. Matthew offered members of his band to the church to provide music. He wanted $1,200 per week.

"That's a lot of money for a new church," Simon responded. "We haven't even met yet."

"I know, man," Simon could hear Matthew's frustration. "These dudes are playing for other churches. They heard you're back and want to play for you, but they need what they are getting now."

Simon was reminded of the business side of the church. He feared that the lack of a strong ministry of music would hurt him down the road. "Man, you know I want to play for you. I told Susan I wished you would leave Shady Grove back in the day when I played for you there. I told her I would play for you if you ever broke off and did your own thing."

"That's deep, man."

"Yeah, I think this is all in God's will. I know the money is a lot, but these guys are the best." Simon agreed to pay the price. It didn't feel good. He decided to not accept a salary to give the ministry a chance to grow. That would offset the cost of the ministry of music. It seemed to be the right thing to do. He had $62,000 in savings with no debt. He would ask the new church to take care of his housing expenses and would find a way to survive until the ministry grew.

Calvin and Simon found a banquet center in the basement of the Northgate Mall. The space was large enough to accommodate 400 people. It would do for now. They purchased a sound system and brought time to promote the new ministry on 103.9/The Light – the gospel radio station.

Simon had to decide on a name. He wanted one that would speak to the theology and purpose of the work. He wanted a name that did more than reflect the identity of a character from the Bible or the location of the church. He was looking to make a statement with the name. He began by developing a mission statement: *We welcome all with the hope that all will welcome Christ into their lives. We believe that Christ's followers should manifest authenticity and a desire for continuous growth. We believe we are a church for children, youth, and adults of all ages. We believe loving relationships should permeate every aspect of church life and that life change often happens in small groups, and that the worship of a limitless God should not be limited to categories. Rather, to express the immensity of God, a diversity of elements and styles seamlessly woven together is necessary.*

"What will define us," he wrote while drinking coffee at the Bean Traders, a coffee house on Ninth Street. "I need to develop a statement about our DNA." He smiled as the words popped onto his Dell computer.

D stands for Definition. Our purpose is to reach out to people who are hurting and lost with the good news of new life in Christ. We desire to meet the needs of all we meet by providing a place for growth, fellowship and service.

N stands for non-negotiable. This is what is essential in this church. Outreach: We warmly welcome all with the hope that all will welcome

Christ into their lives. Spiritual Growth: We believe that Christ's followers should manifest authenticity and a desire for continuous growth. Multigenerational: We believe we are a church of children, youth, adults and senior citizens. Caring Community: We believe loving relationships should permeate every aspect of church life and that life – change often happens best in small groups. Reverent and Relevant Worship: We believe that the worship of a limitless God should not be limited to categories. To express the immensity of God, a diversity of elements and styles seamlessly woven together is necessary. Team Spirit: We believe our greatest impact can be made by teaming together with other churches and ministry organizations to meet the spiritual and physical needs around the corner and around the world.

A stands for Action. To accomplish our purposes and to live out our values, we will give priority to: Vibrant worship services with biblically rooted messages. Bible study groups and spiritual development seminars. Strong children and youth ministries.

Simon backed away from his computer to Review what had been written. He reflected back to all that went wrong with Shady Grove. At the root of it all was a lack of understanding. As he grew, the church remained stuck in an old place – a place where grandma's and grandpa's ways dominated people's perceptions of faith. Simon made the mistake of getting in the way of what formed the faith of those needful of old landmarks.

Simon hoped to do things different this time. He wanted to build a ministry that vowed not to get lost in disagreements, remained committed to bridging the gap caused by age differences, and celebrated the unlimited creativity of those who made up the body of believers.

He would not call people members. They would be called partners, and there would be no list of partners. All who attended became a part by virtue of their presence. Simon wanted to undo the restrictions created by forcing people to affiliate with a band of believers and, in that process, reject the universality of all believers. He wanted to celebrate this group's particularity while pushing people to look past their unique expression of faith.

Simon wanted an authentic community that celebrated the real-life journeys of those who participated. He wanted this ministry to be a place where there was no need to hide. Where people could come out of the darkness of their shame and tell the truth. He wanted it to be a ministry not afraid to go into the shadows. Not afraid to bring light to dark places.

"I still need a name," he whispered to himself as he looked outside at the different people walking down Ninth Street. He watched as a lesbian couple held hands in the middle of the day, and Concrete, a homeless man, stood in silence in his normal spot away from the people sitting in front of the coffee house. He watched a group of high school students make their way to the hill on the other side of the parking lot. One held a guitar and another held a sketching pad.

He watched the mixture of white, black, Hispanic, Asian, gay, straight, rich, not so rich, educated and not so educated share life together. He watched as they celebrated a place where it was acceptable to be free. He had missed this jewel of a place – Ninth Street – a welcoming loving place.

"Damn, this is my church," he chortled still in wait of a name for the new work. "We have to be the light so people like this will feel comfortable. That's it!"

He wrote the words in bold print –THE LIGHT HOUSE. He smiled as he thought of the connections. The light had brought him back to Durham. His first sermon was about that light. Now he would challenge the partners of this new work to become light houses. It all made perfect sense. He was ready for Sunday morning.

"That was an amazing service, Pastor," Chanti said with a big smile. 'God is so good."

"It is so good to be back preaching."

"You need anything, Pastor," Calvin asked. "We have water and Gatorade."

"Thanks, Calvin," Simon smiled. "Gatorade please." The church was packed. Simon knew that many had come just to see what was going on with the new ministry. He saw many of the people from Shady Grove who had fought to terminate him. He held no hard feelings. That was the past. Over 300 showed up to participate in the first service.

Simon preached "A Setback is a Setup for a Comeback." It was based on the story of Joseph who was sold into slavery by his brothers. He endured one bad day after another while contending that God had a desire for him to be a leader. The more he shared his vision, the harder it got for him to achieve it. Jealousy hindered his dreams. Lack of understanding got in his way. He kept pressing.

"We are a congregation of dreams deferred. We are a band of broken spirits. Broken because of setbacks. Lost job. A setback. He won't love you back. A setback. Bills stacked high. A setback. Don't let the setback get in the way of your comeback. It ain't nothing but a setup to the comeback that will be the testimony that will serve as your blessing to others. A setback is a setup for a comeback."

It felt better than old times. Simon felt free to share his faith. There was a warm spirit that lifted him higher. The people kept coming. Some he remembered. Many he was meeting for the first time. Shady Grove had become so big that he never met some of the people. It was one of the things he hated about being part of a large church.

"You remember me," a voice asked from behind him. He recognized that soft tone. It was Patsy.

"Course I remember you, Ms. Hughes. How you doing?"

"Better now that I got my Pastor back," she smiled. His mind took him back to that day in his office. She begged him to take her. Not for her, but for the release of his pain. She kissed him, there in his office, and he kissed back. He touched her warm breast. He kissed her there as she pleaded for him to use her to escape the pain caused by the lions in the den.

He wanted her badly. It was during that hectic week that ended with his exit from the church. He left her wondering what if. What if Jamaica had not showed up during that week to take his attention away from her request? What if Sophie hadn't knocked on the door to end what was sure to happen if only they had a few more minutes to allow the heat to consume more of them?

"You left before I had a chance to say goodbye."

"I know. Everything happened so fast."

"It's not good to leave your friends without saying goodbye."

"Beat me then, Patsy. Can a brother be forgiven?" they laughed.

"Make it up to me later," she slid him her number and walked away before anyone noticed. He felt his heart throb in the same way it did that day in his office. There was a connection that he couldn't fight. Simon watched as she walked away, holding the key to her heart in his hand – a number – 919-699-4657. He placed it in his pocket and smiled at the people while doing his best to get Patsy out of his mind.

MARCH
Vigilance

Anger and humor are like the left and right arm. They complement each other. Anger empowers the poor to declare their uncompromising opposition to oppression, and humor prevents them from being consumed by their fury.
-James Cone-

SIMON FOUND A SEAT IN Duke Gardens near the pond. There he reflected on his life since returning to Durham. It was March now, that special time of year when the plants bloom after the cold of winter. The ducks were on the pond. A couple passed by holding hands and stopped to take pictures of the ducks. It was a day made for romance.

Thoughts of Jamaica were hard to fight. He missed her touch. He missed coming home to her waiting arms every night. He missed making love. He missed strolls in the park while holding hands like the couple taking pictures of the ducks. He listened for the sounds of nature, and prayed that it would be enough to take the loneliness away.

He opened his journal and wrote a poem. He thought of that night at the Washington Duke Hotel. He remembered the thrill of seeing her after so many years apart. Her words seduced him. "I'm not ashamed to tell you what I want," she said that night. "I called you because we had good sex. I want you to take me upstairs and fuck my brains out. After we finish I want to hold you like we did the first time. I'll tell you I love you. I might cry. After we're done we'll go our separate ways. I'll wish I had you every day." He read her words in his journal and remembered how they made love on the floor. They couldn't wait to touch each other. The bed was too far away.

Her touch changed his life. He read the poem he wrote after that night.

You are the reason my heart beats
Jazz tunes and love songs
Melodies with exotic notes
rythmatic themes with
love notes
You are
the reason my vision is swayed by bright tinted colors
paintedby warm hued
brushes on heavenly canvasses that
resemble my heart
You are the taste of sweet kisses dipped in
Hot chocolate wishes coated in spices
found only in my imagination
You are the walk of the ages
the seduction of many nations
the dream of long dead fathers
the envy of determined mothers
the sound locked in hidden spaces
You are the sight the world knew
before the world knew there was
a world to know
You are the taste all taste demands to be
and the color of destiny
You are my last breath
let me be for you
what you are for me
and we will be the taste
of eternity
Come, taste and see

He missed having a woman in his life. For the first time, in a long time, he found himself without a woman there to share space. No wife with children to take care of. No girlfriend to cook dinner for and to share the toil of the day. No woman to gain strength from after each disappointment or to celebrate with after every victory. For the first time he had to carry the burden and cherish the moments alone.

Singleness was difficult for him to carry. Simon craved sex. A month had passed since he arrived in Durham and Patsy's number remained in his wallet. He fought the urge to call her. Not yet, he scolded himself every time he picked up the phone to call her. He held firm to the contention that dating a woman in the church was off limits. He wanted to bring accountability to the work and dating Patsy would compromise the ministry.

He wanted sex, but more than sex he needed to share love. Two birds played in mid air. Two ducks swam side by side. Two dogs ran free from their master's leash in a race for a tennis ball. Two by two they came to the gardens. A man and a woman, holding hands. Two ducks, two birds, two dogs, together to enjoy a picturesque day. He sat alone – without a woman there to kiss. His only company-words written in a journal. Some old thoughts. Some new ones. Words of joy and sadness, hopes and dreams, failures and frustration. He hoped they would keep him satisfied until his queen arrived to sit next to him in the work of the kingdom.

He stood and took a deep breath. Maybe he would go to a movie. Maybe he would treat himself to dinner. Maybe he would go to the Hayti Heritage Center to listen to some spoken word. Maybe he would listen to jazz at The Beyu Café or maybe he would go home and watch a movie. He decided to go to Whole Foods to pick up some squid. He would make himself a calamari salad. After that he would watch TV. Another Friday night date with his best friend– Simon.

They say you are never alone as long as you have Jesus. Bull shit, Simon thought as he pulled in front of Whole Foods. That's no more than a tool used for coping. Simon couldn't hold Jesus. He couldn't enjoy the type of life he wanted with a man long dead. He needed a woman to share space with him, and thoughts of Jesus failed to remove that desire.

"What's up, baby," he flirted with the cashier. "You gonna come over here and give me a hug?" It was part of their daily ritual. She was a cute girl with long locks. If things were different he would ask her out, but he limited conversations to the daily hugs that helped take off some of the edge.

"You know I got some love for you," she stepped out from behind the register and held him firm and long. "You smell so good."

"And you feel so good," Simon was telling the truth. He had to let her go before things got out of control.

"What you cooking tonight, baby?"

"Calamari salad."

"Damn you always cook nice meals. When you having me over?"

"You not getting me in trouble with your baby-daddy," Simon joked to keep things at a distance.

"Baby, daddy can't cook like you"

"Stop tempting me. You know I can use more of those hugs."

"You can have as much as you need, baby. Anytime you ready to cook, I'm ready to hug."

He was saved by the ring of his cell phone. He noticed the number. "Sorry, baby. I got to take this call."

"Go ahead playa. You know where I be," Simon stepped away and walked outside. He picked up after the third ring.

"Hello"

"I miss you, baby," it was Jamaica. "I needed to hear your voice tonight."

"I miss you too. I was thinking about you earlier when I was at Duke Gardens. I read that poem I wrote for you."

"Which one? You wrote me so many."

"The 'You' poem. The one I wrote after we made love that night."

"That's one of my favorites. So, what were you thinking?"

"Hold on, let me put these bags in the car," he hurried to get free from the outside world. He placed the bags in the trunk of his

BMW and found his way to his seat. "I was thinking about how lonely I am without you."

"I know, sweetie. Things were so good. I will never understand why you walked away."

"I can't help you understand. You know I love you."

"I know."

"You know I wish you were here with me."

"You know I wish you would get your black ass down here and take care of me," they laughed to break the intensity of the conversation. He placed his blue tooth in his right ear and headed home to his loft at West Village.

"I would love to come see you, but things are too busy with the church right now."

"I understand."

"You know I want to."

"I know, God needs you more than me."

"That's not true. It's just a messed up situation."

"Are you happy?"

"I'm content. I love the work, but I do miss you. I miss you so much. I wish there was a way to make all of it work together. I wish you were here with me."

"I suppose that's a prayer request."

"It's mine. I hear your frustration, baby."

"I am frustrated. Can I ask you a question?"

"Sure."

"You seeing anyone yet," her question took him by surprise. "Any of those Church ho's got you yet?"

"No. I'm not seeing anyone."

"It's none of my business. I just needed to know."

"Why do you need to know?"

"I need to know where your heart is. I need to know if you have moved on with your life."

"That would be kind of hard to do so fast, don't you think? Come on Jamaica. It hasn't been long enough for me to get involved in a relationship."

"I didn't ask you if you have fallen in love. I asked you if you have fucked one of those Church ho's yet."

"I'm offended by the question."

"Why? It's a good question."

"Because I have to maintain the integrity of my call."

"Does that mean you can't get no pussy because of Jesus? That never stopped us, so why would it stop you now?"

"You weren't a member of the church."

"Got you. So, have you fucked anyone outside the church yet? Maybe I'm asking the wrong question."

"No. I haven't even been on a date."

"That's not healthy. Why haven't you gone out?"

"Damn, Jamaica. What's up with all these fucking questions? It sounds like you want me to fuck someone else."

"I don't want you to, but if you do I understand. Since you left me here by myself I assumed you would find someone else to take care of your needs."

"It's not that easy to move on. I'm looking for more than just sex."

"I'm just saying sometimes you need someone to take the edge off, and if you got someone I understand."

"Is that what you need, Jamaica? Someone to take your edge off? As much as I love sex I'm not looking for that right now."

"You know me, Simon."

"What do you mean I know you?"

"I'm saying you know me. You know what I need."

"Oh I get it. You fucking someone else?"

"Of course I am. You should know that. You went out the front door and I moved someone in the back door."

"You replaced me like that?"

"No, you replaced yourself. I'm saying if you want to come down here and get a little taste of this you can, but I have someone else putting logs in the fire," Simon couldn't believe what he was hearing. He pulled the car on the side of the road next to Brightleaf Square.

"Why you telling me all of this?"

"Because you have a right to know."

"Is it that or is this your way of getting even? Truth is I have no right to know anything. What you do is on you. You're right, I walked away, so why do you feel the need to call me and tell me you're fucking someone else?"

"I needed to let you know in case you decide to come back. You need to know it won't be that easy."

"What makes you think that I was thinking of coming back? Have I said anything to suggest I was moving back anytime soon?"

"You never know with you, Simon."

"What is that supposed to mean?"

"It means you have a way of changing your mind with no warning. You came down here after leaving that church. Then you leave me when everything is going fine. Why wouldn't I think that you might just show up at any time with your damn bags ready to move back in with mommy? Well mommy has moved on. If you want to come down to have sex, that's fine. But I'm moving on with this new man in my life."

"Does he know about me?"

"No."

"But you're willing to continue to have sex with me while being with him?"

"Why not? I still love you. The problem is I don't trust you."

"Will you ever tell him about me?"

"No. He has no need to know."

"Do you love him?"

"I have feelings for him."

"What does that mean?"

"It means I care for him. I trust him with my heart."

"Does he trust you?"

"Yes. I give him no reason not to trust me. We have known each other for a long time."

"How long?"

"Three years."

"You knew him before me?"

"Yes."

"When did you start dating?"

47

"Three years ago."

"Were you seeing him while seeing me?" there was a pause.

"You don't need to know that."

"Yes I do!"

"I stopped seeing him when you moved to Dallas. He moved away for a while and then came back."

"So, you kept contact with him while I was there."

"Yes. But it wasn't like that."

"He had feelings for you while we were together and you didn't tell him about me. How am I supposed to take that?"

"I didn't have sex with him."

"You didn't have to. You kept him on the side just in case things didn't work out."

"Don't be mad."

"Why not! I find out that everything I believed about us wasn't true! Kiss my ass, Jamaica," Simon hung up the phone. For the next hour Jamaica called. He refused to pick up the phone. Instead he cried himself to sleep. He felt like a fool and nothing she said would take that pain away.

He woke up on the couch. Simon didn't fall asleep until after 3:00 a.m. His anger toward Jamaica did not fade his desire to speak to her. He still missed her. He still wished things were different, but now, for the first time, he had to accept that he didn't know her like he thought he did. How could he? They met and connected for a brief time while he was at the University of Missouri. She entered back into his life during that whirlwind week. They made love and shared their love, but was it enough to walk away from the work he loved so much?

His answer was simple. He knew that he did not leave Shady Grove because of Jamaica. His marriage did not end because of her. She provided a place to escape after everything came tumbling down. He needed a place to go, to rekindle and rethink what it meant to live in his skin. Loving Jamaica helped, but had he known the real Jamaica, or was all of it a lie to hide the things she did in the dark?

All along she was waiting for him to leave – to go back to the work he loved. Simon couldn't blame her for fearing the unknown. His life in ministry was a mystery that she could never understand. What bothered him was the game she played while waiting for him to walk away.

It was hard for him to accept it was all a lie, but how could he judge her deception? His love for the church resembled her feelings for the nameless man who made love to her to fill the void left by his absence. As she moaned in his arms, Simon made sermonic cries that helped pacify the despair of those begging to hear his words.

They both played games with their love. His betrayal hid behind the sacred requisites of faith. Hers hid behind a solid wall – one well known by those bitten by the loss of love taken for granted. He assumed she would wait for him. His hope was for her to come to him. His prayer was for a change of mind, a transcendent moment that would have her running into his arms to begin a new life together. It never came. It couldn't come.

He looked at his watch to check the time. It was 9:30 a.m. He reached for his wallet in search of Patsy's number. He needed to get his mind off of Jamaica. It was all so wrong, but he needed it. He needed to see her soon.

"Hello, Pastor," she answered the phone excited.

"A brother can't surprise a sister no more because of caller id," they laughed together.

"A sister needs to know who's calling. It might be a stalker."

"I might have been a stalker calling."

"You know you can stalk me if you want to. And, what has taken you so long to call me? Are you scared of me?"

"Yes, I must be honest. I am scared of you."

"Don't be scared."

"That's easy for you to say."

"Whatever. Life is too short to be scared. You have to live and love. So, what's on your mind?"

"Are you free right now?"

"Sure. What's up?'

"Meet me at the Mad Hatter's in 30 minutes," Simon couldn't believe he made the move. Not only had he asked Patsy to meet him, he asked her to meet him in a public place. "Do you know where it is?"

"Over on Broad Street. I can be there at 10:30."

"Cool," Simon hung up the phone confused over what had just happened. In less than 24 hours his life had transitioned from wanting to be with a woman, but not wanting to because of the demands of his work. Within that short timeframe he had made the call he had fought not to make.

He fought the temptation not to call her back. He didn't want to meet out of pain. He didn't want to drag Patsy into using her to get past being hurt because of Jamaica's actions. He didn't want to use her, like a whiff of cocaine, to cover the pain of rejection. As much as he wanted to see Patsy, he understood how bad it was to call her under these circumstances.

The drive to Mad Hatter's was less than 5 minutes away. He pulled his dreadlocks back into a ponytail that fell to the middle of his back. He splashed on some perfumed oil, put on one of his 7 Diamond shirts and jeans he had purchased from the Gap. He looked through his collection of shoes to find his favorite tan Steve Maddens. He was comfortable with his style – a metro sexual flair with a bohemian twist.

As he walked down the hall of West Village, he thought of all the lonely nights since coming back to Durham. He thought of all those nights, alone, in his loft wondering about Jamaica – wondering if she was thinking about him. He wondered if she missed his touch in the same way he missed hers. If she thought of him making love to her and if she refrained from being with another man because their love was too special to exchange so soon.

His answer came like a bolt of lightning. It hit him void of warning and crushed the innocence of his imagination. He was bamboozled into trusting his heart. So much had been lost along the way. Should he have stayed at Shady Grove and fought to make things better? Should he have spent more time in getting to know

Jamaica before moving to Dallas to be with her? Should he have….?
He stopped himself from contemplating more questions.

He ordered a White Chocolate Mocha and took a seat near the
back of the café/bakery. He pulled out his journal to write a few
lines before Patsy's arrival. He needed time to focus his energy. Time
to reflect on the significance of a year that had appeared as a dream
fulfilled, now unveiled as a nightmare. "Where is the grace in this
God," he whispered a simple prayer. "Your grace is always present.
Show me how this will strengthen me in the end."

He turned his journal to the empty pages and wrote words
intended to release the hurt. "Last night I discovered the truth about
Jamaica. The truth is she has a way of hiding the truth. I'm not
hurt so much because of what she has done with another man; I'm
hurt because she kept him close at hand in case things didn't work
between the two of us. As much as I understand her need to play
it safe, and that I have caused all of this by being uncertain about
things, I had hoped that she loved me enough to believe in us, to
believe in me, even when I struggled to believe in myself.

"I'm hurting today because this all comes a year after Janet left to
be with Maurice Burt. Not only did my wife leave me for a stripper,
he was a member of the church. I preached to that motherfucker
every Sunday. I preached to him while he was fucking my wife. The
deception is painful, and I need rest from it all. I need to feel that
I didn't make a mistake in going to Jamaica, and that I may have
made a mistake in coming back to Durham."

Simon fought being emotional in a public place. The words
Revealed hidden pain. "I feel deceived by the people who have been
close to me. Janet deceived me and left with my children. Sophie
deceived me by taking cash from the deacons to expose a bunch of
lies. I have been surrounded by deception while opening my heart
to the possibility of something greater. Here I stand now, broken by
my trust. I pray that a wall not go up. I pray that I not become so
angry by it all that I forfeit the better part of myself.

"I'm meeting Patsy today. I pray for strength not to move too
quickly. I pray that I not use her to cover all of this pain. I don't
know why I'm here but…"

"Can't you ever let that great mind rest," Patsy stood over him with a smile that lit the room. Her dreadlocks were styled in an updo that brought attention to her hazel colored eyes. Large hoop-shaped earrings dangled from her lobes as bronze shaded lipstick begged for attention. A long multi-colored wrap skirt accented her curvy figure. The orange top matched the red, orange, and yellow in her skirt, and her orange flip-flops were the final touch to the picture of perfection.

"Wow, do you step out of bed looking like that, or have you been working on it since early in the morning."

"That's so sweet."

"No, you know you look good. You know you look good," the laugh broke the tension.

"Would you like something?" Simon stood to hug Patsy. The chemistry was still there. He could feel it in the embrace.

"I really needed that hug," Patsy said. "That feels so good."

They ordered breakfast. He had a vegetarian omelet with whole wheat toast. She had oatmeal with raisins, strawberries, blueberries, brown sugar and cream. They sat and talked. They talked about life at Shady Grove. He talked about Dallas. She talked about her new job at the ad agency. They talked about The Light House. They talked about frustrated love and broken promises.

"Let's get out of here," Simon said. "Would you like to take a ride?"

"Of course," Patsy smiled. It was their chance to get to know one another outside the confines of the church. She wanted to know the man outside of the pulpit. She wanted to know the man who was more than a preacher.

He turned right onto Broad Street, crossing Main Street to get onto Durham Freeway 147. "Where you taking me?" Patsy asked.

"It's a surprise. Sit back and enjoy the ride."

"I love that music. Who is it?"

"Zapp Mama," Simon answered. "I love the way they blend different styles. Sort of like me."

They discussed musical interest. Her love for Hip-Hop was greater than his interest in Jazz. His interest in world music was new to her. They both loved old school R&B. He turned the radio to Foxy-107.1 and they harmonized to Earth Wind & Fire. "That's the way of the world. Plant your flower and you'll grow a pearl. Child is born with a heart of gold. Way of the world make his heart cold."

He veered onto HWY 40 headed in the direction of the airport. He turned right at the exit after the airport, and turned right after that. "You know I'm lost," Patsy said.

"This is one of my favorite getaway places," Simon responded as he turned left to enter Lake Crabtree State Park. His love for water led him to the lake when he first arrived in Durham. He would come after heated fights with Janet to write poetry and meditate.

"How often do you come here?" Patsy asked, as Simon turned right to enter a parking space.

"I try to make it once a month," he turned off the car and got out to open her door.

"Such a gentleman."

"My mama would slap me if I didn't open doors for women," they chuckled again. Simon reached for her hand and led her to a pathway. The short walk down a hill led to an open space near the lake. They were surrounded by a family of trees that served as instruments when the wind blew the leaves. "Let's sit over there," Simon motioned to a gazebo.

A gentle breeze stirred the waters as a man and a boy passed in a boat. A couple held hands on a pier less than 100 yards away.

"It's beautiful here," Patsy was in awe of the place. "I can't believe I didn't know about it before now."

They sat and talked some more. "Why did it take so long for you to call me?" Patsy asked with a hint of disappointment in her voice.

"I had to work through some things first."

"Things like what?"

"It was too soon."

"Too soon to call me? I don't understand that."

"I still have feelings for Jamaica. I didn't want to get caught up in a situation knowing I still care for her."

"You still love her?"

"I do. I love her but I'm hurt because of her."

"She's a fool to let you get away. She should be here with you."

"She has her life back in Dallas. I can't blame her for not wanting to walk away from all of that."

"A good man is hard to find, and you are a good man."

"I have my good and bad, Patsy. You know the man who stands before the people on Sunday, but you don't know me."

"Help me get to know you then."

"It's not that easy. Because you are a partner at the church. I shouldn't be dating a woman in my church."

"Who came up with that crap? If you have feelings for a woman why should you hold back on them because of some stupid rule?"

"It's an ethical thing, Patsy. Like a counselor getting involved with a client."

"If that's how you feel why I am sitting next to you?" she smiled knowing the answer.

"I don't know."

"Yes you do. It's because you can't stay away from me. The vibe is too great to stay away."

"I won't deny that." He reached for her face, touching it gently and then, sitting near the lake where the birds flew in pairs, he kissed her. He felt what had been missing since his return to Durham. His life had been sucked dry by the demands of the work. His lips demanded the passionate taste of a woman's lips. He felt his heart beat again – not from hurt caused by rejection, but from the rhythm of pleasure.

Surrounded by the sounds of the park he heard the melodies of God's creation. The chirping of birds and the bounce of fish as they leaped above water to dive back home. The sound of the wind against the tree limbs calmed the sting of last night's phone call. Simon felt alive again. He held her close. He didn't want to let her go. He wanted to make love, but they both knew it was too soon. They both knew that day would come soon.

APRIL

Mercy • Understanding

For me, forgiveness and compassion are always linked: how do we hold people accountable for wrongdoing and yet at the same time remain in touch with their humanity enough to believe in their capacity to be transformed?
-bell hooks-

THOSE OLD DEMONS HAVE A WAY of coming back when least anticipated. Simon had become comfortable with his move back to Durham. He was at peace from the moment he unearthed the courage to inform Jamaica of his decision. The judgment was confirmed when he walked into that packed room at the public library. The honeymoon was coming to an end. Those old wounds would be reopened to the pouring of spiritual gasoline there to burden Simon again.

There were no conversations about Shady Grove during the early days of his return. The emphasis was on The Light House and the needs of the ministry. The first month was met with excitement. People came in large numbers. The partnership grew to over 400 within 30 days, forcing Simon and the members of the Administrative Team to locate to a new home for the ministry.

They found a building in the Research Triangle Park. The building was part of an industrial complex and it had been the home of Temple of Praise, a Church of God in Christ congregation that was moving into their newly constructed building. The timing was perfect for The Light House and, despite being less than two months old, they had the resources and membership base to justify the relocation.

Simon wasn't afraid of the $4,252 per month lease for the space. His only objection was the location. It was tucked away from public view in an area far removed from inner city woes. Simon wanted to provide ministry within a community that needed the support of a church like The Light House. It was a temporary measure. They moved into the new building on April 13th.

Worship was raw. The casual dress policy gave room for members of the praise team to come void of those sacred costumes that hide the splendor of the human body. Sensuous women sang while maneuvering in ways reminiscent of those late night thrills where lyrics and beats set the stage for a one night encounter. The beauty of the work was in its ability to reach people who felt unwelcome in other churches. Prostitutes, strippers, drug addicts and dealers joined the church and sang with the praise team. They brought the culture and ways of the real world. Simon saw this as reason to celebrate. Others saw it as an offense to God's house.

The same old demons found their way into The Light House. The same demons that ran Simon out of Shady Grove and set him free from the restrictions of black faith were waiting for him at The Light House. The same demons he prayed to exorcise from his work before deciding to come back found him there, gawking at his every move as if in wait for the final blow to his courage. They waited for his tears and frustration to weaken his faith enough to pierce him, one last time, on his weak side.

Simon tried to be free, but his freedom left many looking for something different – something like the old Simon. They craved the familiarity of the days at Shady Grove. They wanted the same choir with the robes draped to their ankles to hide flesh and blood. They wanted nice pictures on the wall reflected in stained glass and a picture of the Messiah behind the choir loft. They wanted a fellowship hall with the smell of fried chicken oozing through the wall in wait of their appetites on Homecoming Sunday.

Their yearning for the traditional outweighed their love for Simon's words. In their minds he became a caricature of faith with his jeans, hip shirts and designer shoes. His dreadlocks scuffled with their old images of the man behind the pulpit. He was too hip for their faith, and following him became too much for them to embrace.

They left in large numbers. The departure began with the controversy of pay for the musicians. It was too much, too soon in the minds of many. It doesn't take all of that to worship God – many said. Simon bit the bullet knowing the criticism was justified. His desire to compete with Shady Grove deprived him of using sound judgment with the ministry of music. It was an opportunity to teach an important lesson; instead he opened the door for a complaint over the very thing he was preaching to change – worship as entertainment.

Simon was tempted to get rid of the band and begin fresh with the ministry of music, but he couldn't because of the relationships he had formed. His friendship with Matthew was growing. Matthew understood the vision, and it was clear he was willing to do all he could to make a difference. He was more than a minister of music. He was a friend and supporter of the vision.

Those demons were eating at Simon. Shortly after the move, things changed. The numbers decreased. The offering decreased. He poured his own money into the work to keep it afloat, but those demons were still at work. The same demons that left Simon crying late at night at Shady Grove came back with a vengeance. This time they brought failure with them. Before it was fear and lust that hindered his focus and frustrated his purpose, but a new enemy had now appeared on the scene – thoughts of failure and regret.

He watched people walk away for the first time. He watched the decline in giving and the look of disgust on people's faces. He questioned his preaching for the first time. He questioned his call and the decision to move back to Durham. It would have been better to stay in that teaching post at the university. It would have been better to find contentment with Jamaica and forget the demands of this work. Those demons were chiseling his spirit – little by little, day by day, Sunday after Sunday – his courage to be was getting harder to preserve.

He sat behind his desk contemplating the meaning of it all. The new building gave the feeling of a growing ministry. The office for the pastor, secretary office, lobby, kitchen and sanctuary with 600 seats symbolized movement in the right direction. It all looked good on the outside, but the people were leaving. There was something about the work that wasn't catching hold.

He closed his eyes for one last prayer before leaving. The mid-week Bible study had helped give him strength for another day. He rose from his seat to leave the empty building when the phone rang.

"The Light House."

"Hey Daddy," it was Carmen. "I miss you!"

"I miss you too, baby," a smile replaced the frown of frustration that had consumed the past hour. "What you doing tonight?"

"I got my results from my PSAT," he could tell from the tone of her voice the score was high. "Wanna know how your Sugar Baby did?"

"Had to be good. You know you got your daddy's brains," he laughed.

"Daddy. I got a 2300," with that score she would be recruited by schools across the country. "Who the boss, daddy? Who the boss?"

"Sugar Baby the boss," the two clowned like old times. A tear escaped his eye as the pride of the accomplishment consumed him. He had often feared that Carmen and Chris would suffer due to the divorce but both continued to do well academically. Chris would enroll at Northwestern in the fall and planned to major in journalism and play football. He was the star running back on his high school football team, and was second in his class academically. Carmen wanted to go to Princeton before heading to medical school.

"I'm on my way, daddy."

"You know I'm proud of you, baby. You have always made me proud. I wish you were here with me. I miss you so much."

"I Love you too, daddy. Just get your butt up here to see us soon. You coming for Chris's graduation next month?"

"I'll be there."

"Here's Chris. Hold on," she passed the phone on to her brother. Things had been tense between Simon and Chris since the divorce was final in January. Chris was angry because of Jamaica. He understood the divorce. He had to. His mother left his father for another man, and now she was pregnant with Maurice's child. Chris didn't like Maurice and blamed Simon for not putting an end to his mother's bad decision to move.

"What's up, pops?"

"Everything is great with me. You ready for that big day?"

"Yeah. The coaches want me to take classes over the summer to get me used to campus."

"That sounds like a winner. You going to do it?"

"I'm going to take two classes. That way I won't have to be so stressed with a big load the first semester. Coach says he doesn't want to red shirt me because they need me to play right out the box."

"That's alright, son."

"I want to play, but I had hoped to have a red shirt year to give my body a chance to grow some more and to build an academic foundation," Chris was wise beyond his years. Simon smiled, knowing his son had everything under control. "So, I can get on campus and pump some iron and really get in the books."

"It sounds like you have it all figured out."

"There's one problem, pops."

"What's that?"

"I wanted to spend the summer with you," Simon was shocked to hear Chris say that. "I mean you the one who helped me become a man. I needed to get some things right inside before taking this big step."

"I wish you could do that. I know I miss you."

"I know. Well, I felt it was a good time to do it since you left that woman."

"You mean Jamaica?"

"That woman. I didn't like her, pops. I'm glad you left her,"

"I didn't know that."

"She didn't like us, pops," this was news to Simon. "She treated us like we got in her way. She acted like she couldn't wait for us to leave."

'Why didn't you say something?" Simon felt ashamed that he never noticed.

59

"You was too in love to listen, pops. Just like moms is too in love to listen."

"Your moms got things under control," Simon still respected Janet as a great mother and didn't want to feed into a negative conversation. "You know she loves you."

"Whatever pops? You know Mo ain't nothing but a gold digger. He followed moms because she got that good job over at the university and he ain't even got a degree. How am I supposed to feel about him being with my moms and he hasn't done half of what I have? How am I supposed to respect him for being a bum?"

"Your mother must see something in him."

"I know pops. That's what pisses me off. She sees how good he can make her feel," Chris's anger was coming out.

"You know I can't let you disrespect your moms like that. How would you feel if someone else said that about her?"

"I know, pops. She needs to check her shit. Sorry, pops. She needs to check herself," it was the first time Simon heard his son curse. It was a sign that his boy was growing up. He was hurting and needed the wisdom of his father. He felt free enough to share how he felt.

"Sometimes people make mistakes because of pain, Chris. I have made my share of them. I made a mistake with Jamaica. I wish things were different with me and your moms so that you wouldn't have to deal with all of this. The good thing is it hasn't messed you up. You have a football scholarship. You have great grades and we are talking."

"I know, pops. This all pisses me off. I'm going to have a brother or sister who has that jerk as a father. Man, that pisses me off!"

"I know. Tell you what. Ask your moms if I can take you somewhere after graduation. We can spend a week together to reconnect before you go to summer school."

"Dig that"

"Cool. Let me know soon so I can plan a nice trip."

"Let you know tomorrow."

"One last thing, Chris."

"What, pops?"

"Don't you ever hold your feelings back again. If you have something to say, say it. If you don't like something I'm doing, or if you don't like someone I'm with, you tell me. I may not change things, but at least we can talk it through. You hear me?"

"I do. This stuff is hard, pops."

'I know. It's hard for all of us, but we still have each other. As crazy as things are we will always be family. Nobody, nothing can change that. You my boy. I love you and I'm proud of you not because you the big time football star headed to Northwestern, or because of that GPA. I'm proud of you because you have become a great man. You got that?"

"Love you, pops. Sorry for cussing."

"It's okay. Preachers cuss too."

"I know. I heard you do it," they laughed. "In that case. I'm sorry for being an asshole."

"In that case, I'm sorry for being with an asshole."

"Carmen! Get on the other line!"

"Hey, pops," Carmen said. "We love you!"

"We love you, pops," Chris said. They hung up leaving Simon in his chair drenched with tears. This time they were tears of joy.

"Thank you Jesus for restoring my relationship with my son. Thank you Jesus!"

Simon rushed to pick up the remaining items he needed to cook dinner for Patsy. "Give me a pound of shrimp and a half pound of scallops," he requested. "I'll be over in produce."

He needed just a few more items for the ceviche– a lemon, lime, cucumber, chives, tomato and cilantro. He grabbed what he needed and placed them in his hand-held basket. The shrimp and scallops were waiting for him when he returned. "Thanks bro," he motioned to the man who prepared his seafood.

"Anytime, Pastor," he made his way to the vitamin section. He needed some borage oil. He was reaching for a bottle when a familiar voice attacked his spirit.

"Brother Pastor. Heard you was back," He turned to meet the evil glare of Deacon Andrews, the man who led the charge to destroy his life and work at Shady Grove.

"Deacon Andrews," he did his best to be pleasant. The year had aged the deacon and Simon kept in mind the need to respect the lives of the elders. "How are things with you?"

"We're making it the best we can. My wife told me to come to this place to pick up some flax seed oil. She said the stuff is good for you."

"She's right. It helps fight high blood pressure and increases your energy. Since when has your wife been into alternative medicine?"

"She's been meeting with this woman who says it helped change her life. She got into it after getting out of the hospital." Simon had heard that Mrs. Andrews had been sick a lot after the fiasco at the church. Learning that her husband was a pedophile was hard to deal with. She left him for a while, but came back when things began to fall apart in her own life.

"I'm glad to hear she's getting better," Simon always liked Mrs. Andrews. It was her judgmental husband he hated so much.

"I hear things are going good at the new church," the shift to talk about the church made Simon uneasy.

"It's hard work starting a new work. It will take time for us to get it were it needs to be, but with Christ, all things are possible."

"You have our prayers. You know we love you." No, Simon thought, I don't know you love me. How can you say that after all you did to tear my life apart? That's what he thought as he smiled and pretended that everything was fine. It wasn't. Simon felt deep hatred. The type that wishes bad things for others – things like sending them to Hell. Things like lightning bolts and fire to help them understand that you cannot touch God's anointed vessel. He kept smiling as the hypocritical bastard acted as if nothing ever happened.

You should be in jail for what you did to Carmen, Simon thought as he watched those dusty lips flap nonsense in the air. You should burn in Hell for taking advantage of a child and for standing before God's people as if you were the model of Christianity. He wished the heavens would open and a loud voice would pronounce "this is an old asshole in whom I am disgusted completely." He wished

God would tell the world the truth whenever the old fake deacon walked into a room. Simon smiled, but felt the urge to slap him in his face.

Simon stood and listened. He waited for those words to flow from the old man's lips. Those simple words would have set Simon free to love the bastard again. "I'm sorry" he waited and hoped for those words. "I'm sorry for mistreating you" he kept waiting and waiting. They didn't come. Simon knew they never would. The old deacon's pride would not allow him to admit a mistake. In his mind he was justified for all his wrongdoing.

"The evil bastard thinks his shit don't stink," Simon thought as Deacon Andrew told the story of a trip he and his wife had taken to Asheville.

"Have you met our new pastor yet?" Andrews asked.

"No, I haven't, but I've heard good things."

"He's doing good work."

"Good. My prayers are with the church. I have a deep love for the work there and want to see the church thrive," Simon wanted to believe it, but his competitive edge wished the church would be cast into the lake of fire for what they had put him through.

"Well, Brother Pastor, you stay in touch with us."

They departed with a handshake. The encounter stirred emotions concealed by pretension. Simon hurriedly left the store to get home to think about more important things- like cooking dinner for Patsy He focused on cooking to take his mind off the pain of the past.

"You weren't kidding when you said you can cook," Patsy said after tasting the shrimp and scallop Ceviche. "I was thinking you might serve some Hamburger Helper. This is gourmet."

"A woman like you deserves better than Hamburger Helper," Simon responded after sipping wine – Melini Orvieto, an Italian white. "Cooking is one of my passions."

"What are some of your other passions?"

"You."

"Right answer. Keep that up and I might have to serve you me for desert," Simon loved Patsy's forwardness. It was one of the things that reminded him of Jamaica.

"I'm certain it will taste good," he smiled playing along with the flirting game. For the past two weeks the game of words had dominated their relationship. Simon failed to make the move that they both were waiting for. Something kept him from touching her in the way he did that day in his office. A wall was up.

"Don't play with me, Simon," she moved before he had a chance. She took control, like that day in his office. She moved away from the table to get closer – much closer. She walked in his direction from the other side of the table slowly, touching her body indicating the erroneous zones. One there – her breast. Another there – her inner thigh. Yet another there – the tip of her lips.

Coltrane's groove set the ambiance for what would follow. "I've had enough of that," she whispered. "I need some of this." She touched the side of his face as she straddled his lap. She kissed the side of his neck as he made waves in the middle of her back.

"You feel so good," Simon's body ached for the stroke of a woman's love. "You feel so good."

"I've always wanted you, Simon. I wanted you long before that day when I came into your office. I told you I wanted to be what you needed to get away from all the pain. I feel your pain when you preach. I feel it when you look at me. I know you want me. I know you're scared, but you don't have to be. I'm safe. I need you as much as you need me and no one needs to know what we do in the dark."

It was the same offer made long ago. Before he was surrounded by holy relics to dampen the mood. Before there was the knock at the door to end that tender moment. His thirst for her never ended, it was subdued for a season as he played games with Jamaica. Time failed to cease the deep attachment of their heated bodies. Their bodies matched and moved like the tango. Their forbidden desire found space for uninhibited expressions. His whimper danced with each moan she made. Together they danced the dance of lovemaking.

He kissed her there. In return she kissed him there. He held her in that special way, and she held him in the way he favored – without words of command, she knew, he knew what it took to please the other. They found the peak together as each breath formed a greater union. As she cuddled the pain away with each movement she made, he felt the release of demons at the beginning of each stroke. Up, gone are the memories of Jamaica. Down, gone is the pain of Shady Grove. Up, forgotten is the feeling of failure that consumes each day. Down, lost is the regret of walking away.

He couldn't say I love you. He felt an undeniable connection, but not love. Not yet. An overwhelming mood of pleasure, but not love – not yet. He held her close at the end of it all. It was more than he expected. It was less than he had hoped. He wanted the soft caress of her warm body to take the ache away. It did. He wanted having her next to him after making love to remove all memories of Jamaica. It didn't.

He held her tight hoping the thoughts of another woman would go away. He imagined making love with Jamaica. He remembered, again, the night they touched at the Washington Duke Hotel. There, on the floor, he told her he loved her. He wished they could be together. He wished they had never strayed from one another. He said all of that after making love.

He wanted to feel the same way again. He wished those words – I love you – would come easy with Patsy. The guilt of making love without being able to say it stripped him of the pleasure of the moment. He envisioned Jamaica's face. He wondered why she couldn't be with him after he shared his dream of coming back to Durham. His mind played games as he held Patsy in his arms, games after making love in a way reserved for those who can say those words – I love you.

"That was so good," Patsy moaned to confirm his suspension. That she too enjoyed making love. "Can we do it again?"

He smiled to fight the face in his imagination. The lure of Jamaica's memory forged a high partition separating two hearts. Their bodies blended to create new exotic taste. Their moans echoed like compositions scripted by one of the masters. They made love again and again. They made love void of those words to enunciate the ending to what appeared as a perfect night. Their bodies shielded the truth. The energy of their connection kept silent the truth of the moment. There was no love. Not yet. Only great sex to cover the agony of the past.

They woke up the next morning to the sound of Herbie Hancock's project *Gershwin's World*. Hancock's delicate touch of the piano keys helped pave the way for intimate touch. The flicker of the candles strategically placed to mingle lights and shadows exposed Patsy's naked body draped across the silk sheets. The smell of burning oils added to a mood that needed no more than two willing participants.

There was something magical there. Something that words could not express, yet Simon could not find the words. He knew them well, but forced them back as he pondered the last dance with those words. He kept them locked in that place reserved for pain. She looked at him as if in wait for words to illustrate the night.

"Tell me what's on your mind, Simon," she kissed his chest to press the conversation.

"I'm thinking that was awesome," he wished he could say more. He was hoping she didn't need more.

"No kidding. That was beyond awesome. Our bodies were meant to be together," he knew that to be true. Making love with Patsy was better than ever before. Better than with Jamaica. The thought slipped in the middle of reflecting about the night. Jamaica popped up again. This time in a moment of comparison, but Patsy's touch was more intense. The thought shocked him.

"No woman has ever made love to me the way you do," the words articulated the feelings associated with the night. They were different than I love you. Not as meaningful as those other words, but they provided the context for the beginning of something new. Something different and more meaningful than anything that had come before. No one has ever made love to me the way you do were words that began the rise of a new bold adventure. It would be one that held close the truth of its beginning no one has … not even Jamaica.

MAY
Wisdom •Mother Earth •Adaptability

I imagine one of the reasons people cling to their hates so stubbornly is because they sense, once hate is gone, they will be forced to deal with pain.
-James Baldwin-

THE BRIEF MEETING WITH Deacon Andrews exposed a weakness that Simon didn't want to admit. He had not forgiven Andrews and some of the other members at Shady Grove. His hatred uncovered a vulnerability that would attack his soul if not checked. It would eat at his peace and rob him of all his joy. He would feel the anger stirring like the vomit of intoxication every time he saw a member of the church. Each conversation would leave him empty and wondering about his role in the waning of the ministry.

The ministry was fading. The initial excitement died away shortly after the move to the larger building. Some of the faithful had left Simon with the task of rebuilding a work that needed capable leaders to share the load. Simon had poured his own resources into the work hoping things would come around. His savings was rapidly declining and he wasn't receiving a salary to recoup what was lost.

The face of Deacon Andrews and the members of Shady Grove haunted him. That Thursday night meeting crept into his spirit to remind him of his departure. Simon questioned his decision to walk away. The hard work was done after the church voted to allow him to stay. He could have kept pressing through the problems at the church after Deacon Andrews was exposed for violating Carmen.

Her courageous statement before the church shocked people into rethinking things they had said about Simon. He could have stayed and fought through the problems, but he moved to Dallas to be with Jamaica.

Simon was tempted into blaming her for his actions. He made the sacrifice to be with her, and once he did she didn't want to be with him. He slapped himself back into reality whenever he thought that way. He left her to come back. It wasn't Jamaica who made the decision to leave Dallas – he did. It was the unknown that had him obsessed. How could Jamaica pretend to feel the way she did when there was another man in the waiting? Did she really love him or was it all a part of a game she played to get what she wanted from him? Did she want his warm body in her bed at night? Did she want the meals he cooked and the benefits that come with a highly educated man-income, acclaim and validation? Did she want the stares of others when they walked together? Did she love the attention having him in her life brought, or did she really love him?

The root of Simon's pain was not Jamaica. It was not the memory of Deacon Andrews. Simon's ache was attached to the throb of feeling like a failure. Success would have covered the sting of Jamaica's confession, and it could be used as a spear in the heart of those who questioned Simon's leadership. It could have served as the 'I told you so' to silence all of his critics. Failure stared him in the face, forcing him to contend with his decision to move back into the ministry and the tight chains wrapped around his potential freedom.

Simon was afraid of failure. For the first time he was witnessing his work not being received by those who came to hear him preach. The swagger was gone. His newfound freedom had lodged a divide between his voice and the expectations of the people. His freedom confused them. It made it difficult for them to comprehend what it means to be a person of faith. He challenged them to think. They wanted to be told how to live, what to think and what to do.

Freedom strikes an unsettling nerve for those unprepared to be free. Freedom demands accountability. It takes the power away from the religious demigods they had become accustomed to worshipping.

The self-made bishops of the airwaves stripped them of their freedom by handing them a way of faith that denounced the worth of the human spirit. They were chained by the assumptions of faith. They sought the keys to the kingdom while the door was found within. They prayed and hoped for proof of their faith – some material evidence of God's love for them – while refusing to embrace the love God Revealed in every step they take.

Freedom required a new journey. The quest for finding meaning in the world of material good is replaced with a movement toward finding meaning from within the human spirit. Simon was disturbed that people were enslaved by the enticements of the material world. He challenged them to let it go, to find true meaning by embracing the world of the spirit versus finding value by fulfilling the expectations of others to prove their worth.

They weren't ready to be free. They preferred the enslavement to debt and pleasure. They left because they wanted words to conform to their vision of meaning. They wanted a message that endorsed the American Dream. They wanted that prosperity message that provided the keys to success exposed in the Word of God. They wanted Simon to help them get rich and to make them feel good about their obsession with the things of this world.

Simon taught a different message. It was his contention that prosperity theology is guilty of sin. The sin is in the assumption of human worth couched in material goods. It rejects the Biblical injunction to denounce the things of this world, to pick up the cross and follow Christ. In denying both the Biblical and historical interpretations of the work of the Church, prosperity thinkers have created a world of division that is the rich versus the poor, the enlightened versus the weak minded, and the blessed versus the cursed.

They weren't prepared to look behind their specific culture and how it swayed their interpretation of truth. Simon argued most of what we hold true in reference to faith is no more than an American interpretation juxtaposed against the words of our faith. The American Dream becomes the Christian way. Our worship of America as the validation of Christian principles negates the truth of how God has functioned and continues to move around the globe. America's truth is not God's truth for the world. It's the truth of how God has moved within America, and can't be used as a way of defining how God moves in other parts of the world.

Their inability to embrace freedom forced Simon to rethink his own claims. His freedom was at risk due to the hard work in moving people toward their own liberation. More and more, Simon found himself hiding from his own freedom. The conversation with Deacon Andrews reminded him of the burden carried when under attack by God's folks. He remembered the rumors and gossip. He remembered the shame he carried and the worry that loaded him down.

Things would be different if the people were free, but their lingering in oppression meant he could not be free alone. He needed their unconditional love to be free. He feared their words again. Those harsh words of judgment about the way he lived his life pounded at his memory and mandated a reconsideration of each position made. He feared losing more than he had. More money. More members. More security. More happiness. More love.

The locust had come and sucked life away again. He was back to that former place where freedom could not be found due to the strains of living the faith. He was back to pain and sorrow. Back to not being sure about his work and fearing what people had to say. Back to the slide leading to death. His move back to Durham was his backslide. His movement back to the church was his relapse to frustration.

He feared being seen out with Patsy. What would the people think if they knew he was dating a member of the church? He feared their judgment. He feared more leaving because of his desire to be happy again. He gave them power to control his joy. They owned his happiness. His fear of them kept him entrapped behind the doors of their expectations. Seeing Deacon Andrews took him there. It reminded him of what can happen when people get stuck in the middle of your business. His freedom gave him space to function void of fear, but now the anxiety of potential failure took him back to that place where preachers walk on eggshells and function with one eye looking to see who is looking.

"We have to do something about the ministry of music," Steve suggested. "People have a hard time understanding why we're spending so much money for music." Steve and the people were correct in their assessment. Simon decided to bring in the band to compete with the ministry of music at Shady Grove. He feared people would be turned off by an upstart ministry that lacked the energy of worship that had become the norm at Shady Grove. At the root of Simon's decision was his fear that his preaching and teaching would not be enough to keep the people coming back.

"Matthew has already agreed to take a pay cut," Simon added. The Administrative Team was meeting to discuss a way to continue to pay the rent after the decline in attendance. "Maybe we need to let the other band members go." It was a tough decision, but one that had to be made. Paying a drummer, two people playing the keyboard and a bass guitar player was too much for a dying church to uphold.

Simon was saddened by the need to terminate the services of the other band members. With actions being taken to minimize cost, the church was going backwards instead of forward. Simon was aware that he made a mistake by moving into the new location too soon, and he had failing to give the ministry time to formulate an identity before adding to the work. Simon had bought into his own press clippings. His arrogance had come back to harm the work of the church.

He believed his words would draw thousands to the church. He believed they would come in droves and, once there, they would find others ready to do the same. They did come, but not for this new free version of the Preacha' Man, but for the one locked in and oppressed by the conceptions of Shady Grove's leadership.

Simon remembered the day he bowed his head and cried after feeling like a failure. Shady Grove was a church on the decline. Membership was fading after he was hired to replace the previous pastor. He bowed his head and prayed, "Lord forgive me for not being good enough."

He wiped the tears from his eyes and raised his head. Before him stood 15 people prepared to join the church. What appeared as failure was God teaching Simon a lesson – he couldn't take credit for success in ministry and he couldn't take blame for what seemed to be failure. God was working even in the appearance of failure.

From that day the membership at Shady Grove grew beyond anyone's imagination. 25 people joined on the following Sunday. 20 more joined the week after that. They kept coming until Shady Grove grew to mega Church status. It grew faster than Simon's ability to adjust to the demands of growth. It came with a price – they placed him on a throne reserved for God. They envisioned him as the incarnation of God's work on earth, and, in doing so, failed to understand their role in building the kingdom of God.

The people didn't love Simon - they loved the false representation that stood before them each week. They wanted that back. They left looking for the former version of Simon – a preacher in a nice suit, with a humorous message and who would help them feel better about their narrow minded conception of existence.

"I hate to say it, but we need to get out of this lease," Chanti added. "I love it here but we can't afford to stay. We need to be thinking of a way to pay you, Pastor."

"We need to develop some stability," Simon said. "We moved into this location with the thought that we needed it for growth. Now we are struggling to survive because of a building. I never wanted us to become slaves to a building. It's not teaching good stewardship."

"So, what do we do with this lease?" Steve asked.

"I can take a look at it for loopholes," Mary, an attorney offered. Mary had been a faithful member of Shady Grove. She was there when the church exploded and became the model for ministry in Durham. She, like so many others, waited for Simon to perform magic one more time.

"Keep in mind the lease is in my name," Simon added. "Remember they didn't want to put the lease in the name of the church because we were just getting started. If it means I have to take the hit for bad judgment, I'll take it."

"We would hate for you to have to do that," Steve added. "After everything we did to get you here, we owe it to you to not have you go through that."

"You don't need to feel bad about my coming back to Durham. I did so because I believed it is what God wanted me to do. I still believe this is what God wants."

"I know that's right," Steve responded. "The one thing I can say is your preaching is more powerful than before." Simon wished he felt the same. His confidence was in pause mode as the church worked through the business side of things.

"Amen," Mary chided in with a high five for Steve. "Don't let this get you down, Pastor. Our lives have been changed by The Light House. Some people ain't ready for this thunder, but God is in it. The Lord is working in you, Pastor. Don't you question that."

The decision was made to move The Light House in 30 days. Steve would contact the school system about holding worship in one of the schools. It was a tough move to make, but it was time to be free from a lease that was strapping the church of all its resources. The group prayed for peace and understanding. Simon prayed for the pain to go away.

"I still don't understand why I can't go with you to the graduation." Things between Simon and Patsy were getting tense. Her demand to be more central to his life was making it harder for him to process through a variety of issues. "I can come back to Durham after the service."

"It doesn't make sense for you to fly up there and then come back on your own," Simon said.

"Why not? I travel all the time. It's not like I'm not used to taking a short term trip. It's not like Chris and Carmen don't know me. They remember me from Shady Grove."

"It's one thing for them to remember you as a member of the church and another for them to meet you as the woman who is dating their father."

"Come on, Simon, they are old enough to deal with that. Besides with all the shit Janet has put them through they should be ready for this."

"Just because their mother has introduced them to some crazy shit doesn't mean I should do the same. Those kids have gone through enough without having to deal with their daddy's shit again."

"So this is about the old stuff. When will you forgive yourself for Jamaica? You have a right to have a woman by your side."

"Jamaica hurt them. What they need right now is to have me for themselves without a woman on my arm. There comes a time when a man has to be man enough to take care of what his children need."

"You sound like they are babies, Simon. They're 15 and 17. Give me a fucking break."

"All I know is I'm not ready to introduce another woman into my children's lives. Things have to be different before I go there again."

"Like things will have to be different before you let the church folks know about us? Huh! Is it the same shit that keeps you from letting those motherfuckers rule your life? When you gonna go out in public with me? If it's enough for you to fuck me behind closed doors, why can't you take me out in a public place and let the people see us together?"

"I have too much to lose, Patsy. I have lost too much already and I'm not taking that risk right now. Everything has fallen apart in my life. I'm not ready to risk what's left."

"'I don't get that!"

"You don't get how I'm struggling now because of the crap I've been through. I walked away from Shady Grove thinking it was worth it all, and when I did I discovered Jamaica was playing game on me. You don't get how I lost a six-figure income with all the perks for this shit. You think this is what I signed up to be when I made the sacrifices to be trained to be the best at what I do."

"You have to forgive yourself for all of that and live, Simon."

"How can I live when everything is falling apart? The church is dying a slow death. People I thought loved me and my work have given up and moved on to other churches. Fuck, people I believed loved me have gone back to Shady Grove. I don't know what or who to trust anymore. Think about that, Patsy."

"What's that got to do with my loving you, Simon? Why should we suffer because of all of that? Don't you have a right to a life?"

"I have to build things back up, Patsy. I have to prove to the people that I'm not what they say I am. People think I'm a womanizer. I have to live my life to prove them wrong."

"So, you have to stop living so you can prove to those assholes that you aren't what they say you are? Do you hear how stupid that is, Simon? You are living your life for other people. Is that what God wants with your life, that you put yourself in the box they made for you so you can jump in it and do what they say you should do? Is that the freedom you preach to us about, or is that just for the rest of us? What about you, Simon? I love you because you fight to be free, or at least I thought you fought to be free."

"I'm sorry my career matters to me. I care that my work won't be lost because of the way people think about me."

"People can't take your ministry from you, Simon. Only you can do that. People shouldn't make your life for you. Your life belongs to you, not them. You have given them power over you and I'm in the middle of it all, suffering because you are playing the damn church game all over again!"

"You told me it didn't matter to you, Patsy."

"What you mean I told you it didn't matter?"

"When we hooked up you said this was about how you would be there for me. That you wanted to help me get through the pain. Now you talking like a woman in search for more than that."

"That's because I have feelings now that I didn't have then! Give me a break! I was happy in the beginning to have a casual relationship. How was I to know that I would fall in love with you? Are you punishing me for falling in love? Are you punishing me because of what all the other women did to hurt you, Simon? Am I paying the price for Janet's affair and Jamaica's deception? Am I having to suffer because of your other bitch – the church and all she has done to fuck up your life?" The rage had taken over. Patsy's tears told the rest of the story. Not only did she love Simon, it hurt her watching him hurt himself because of all that had happened.

"I'm sorry for being scared," Simon reached over to embrace Patsy. "I have to work through all of this on my own." She cried in his arms. For the first time Simon felt something different between the two of them. He felt sorrow for how she felt and his inability to get past his fears. More than that, he felt love. He knew then, while she cried in his arms, that he loved her.

"I just wish you could be free," she said.

He took hold of both of her hands, forcing her to look him in the eyes. "Patsy, I know this is hard, but you need to know this. I love you. I do love you. Be patient with me please. This is not easy for me, but I do love you."

She looked at him shocked at his words. It was the first time those words parted his lips. She had said them over and over, but he reserved them for this moment. She knew they had meaning, and she felt the energy behind the sound of his voice. I love you helped her find peace in that moment. Peace enough not to hurt too much over not being able to witness the graduation of his son. Enough to help her get through another week of being kept behind closed doors.

The entire family was present to celebrate Chris's graduation. It had been a while since Simon had seen his parents. They carried the typical grandparent's pride that came with witnessing the rite of passage of one of your own. Chris wore the yellow rope around his neck indicating his academic excellence. He epitomized the scholar athlete. He had made it, despite two years of family instability.

Simon was second-guessing his decision not to allow Patsy to come. Watching Janet hold Maurice's hand tugged at his heart. No, he no longer had feelings for her. His pain was related to how she escaped the controversy void of scars. She didn't lose work or children, money or reputation. She moved away, and stayed away from the glares of those waiting to launch darts at her character. He envied her ability to stay away from Durham. Her life in Chicago provided all the comforts she had become accustomed to over the years.

He watched as Maurice rubbed her swelling belly. She was six months pregnant. No wedding was planned, but the two lived together under the same roof as his teenage children. The thought of a man who had stripped for a living nurturing his children troubled Simon. The words of his son reminded him of how fragile youth can be. His mind told him he made the right decision in keeping Patsy away from the drama of the day. His heart needed love by his side to protect him from the ache coming from all directions.

Patsy's presence would have required Simon to ponder the contradictions of his own claims. He fought for his right to be free from cultural norms and restrictions while being critical of the relationship between his ex-wife and a former stripper. Simon knew that a verbal assault of Janet's relationship with Maurice opened the door for an attack on his past relationship with Jamaica and his current bond with Patsy-a member of the church.

Simon sat next to Carmen. Her smile denoted a deep love and admiration for her big brother. The two had supported each other through the separation and divorce of their parents, the move away from friends to a new city, the unholy union between their mother and Maurice, and their father's fascination with an intensely sexy woman. They carried each other through the hard days, parenting one another and encouraging the other when it felt like the weight of the world was falling on top them.

"That's my brother! That's my big brother," Carmen screamed as Chris received the piece of paper validating his release from high school. "Go big brother!" Simon couldn't help but cry. The guilt consumed him; pride lifted him. He felt the guilt of not being present for the end of the battle to help his son get to the other side. Guilt for caring more about his own love life, and not being present to help Carmen and Chris work through falling in love for the first time and the first time their hearts were broken. He felt the guilt from not being present when the first acceptance letter came in the mail, and when Chris worked through which college he would decide to attend.

He wanted to be more than a once a month child support check. His role as their father didn't end with separation, it wouldn't end with graduation. There's was a bond for life, for their common blood forged a union even deeper than the one with their mother. He wished he could have been more for them. He looked forward to the week they would spend together.

The service came to an end with the tossing of caps. Chris made his way to the family to receive his congratulatory hugs and well wishes. Simon waited to give everyone a chance to greet Chris. Carmen was the first to jump in his arms. His mother was next to soak his robe with tears. Grandma and Grandpa embraced the boy who once crawled in their living room, pulling special figurines on the floor as he went along. It was hard to believe time had passed so fast. In the twinkling of an eye, a boy had grown up to become a man.

"I'm so proud of you, baby," Grandma Doris cried as she hugged her grandson.

"Thanks, grandma," Simon smiled, happy to see both sets of grandparents present. Eugene and Grace, Janet's parents, made their way to hug Chris.

"Proud of you too, dog," Maurice said, proving his lack of class. Simon nodded in disgust.

"Thanks," Chris responded doing his best to show respect.

Simon stood waiting for everyone to finish greeting Chris. "Hey pops," Chris beamed in stark contrast to the way he greeted Maurice. It served as a code between the two of them after the conversation earlier in the month. They hugged and cried to consecrate the rekindling of their bond. The years had sent them both in different directions, and both missed their special linkage.

"Chris, I was sitting there thinking of how much I have missed this past year. I missed your football and basketball games. I missed watching you run track. I missed our father to son talks," Simon had decided to be real in this moment. He wanted this moment to be one that Chris would always remember. "I missed so much during your last year in high school, but I'm thankful that you had enough in you to survive it without my being there."

"Thanks, pops. You gave me enough during those first 16 years to last a lifetime," he hugged him again. "I'm so glad you're here."

"And thank God Maurice was there to be a strong role model in your absence," Janet blurted to the amazement of everyone. Doris looked at Janet with a scorn that warned her to back off.

"I can't wait for our trip, pops," Chris showed the wisdom of a man who had experienced chaos in the making. "Where you taking me?"

"I'm taking you to Arizona. I'm taking you to a place called Sedona. There are some things there I want to show you before you go to Northwestern."

"Ain't never heard of no Sedona," Maurice said.

"I'm not surprised," Doris responded. "They probably don't have strip clubs."

"What you trying to say," Maurice lashed back. "You don't know me like that."

"I think I already said it and I'm glad I don't know you like that," it was time for a truce but Chris pulled Simon to the side to laugh at the exchange.

"Grandma is a trip, pops," Chris giggled as they walked to the parking lot.

"You have to love her," Simon couldn't fight back the laughter. Everyone knew about Maurice's work as a stripper. It became part of the conversation in Durham after Simon left Shady Grove. Chris called his grandmother to share his feelings about his mother not only dating but moving in with a man who she met at a strip club.

"You handled it well, Chris," Simon said.

"I can't let all of that mess up this day, pops. God has been good to me and I just want to stay focused on what is important. Feel me."

"I do."

"That's why I wanted to spend some time with pops before going off to school. There's some things that I have to get rid of before I move on."

"That's really mature, Chris."

"Naw, it's not what you think, pops. You learn to look past some things when you make mistakes. I've made a few and," Chris paused to collect his thoughts. "I don't know what to do about my mistake, pops." He became emotional. Tears started to flow as he shared his pain. "I got my girl pregnant, pops. Cheryl is two months' pregnant."

"Dang, I ain't never seen anything like this before," Chris sat in amazement at the stunning array of red sandstone formations that make Sedona, AZ, America's most beautiful city. The red rock appeared to glow in dazzling orange and red as the sun set. Simon and Chris viewed the splendor of the rocks while sitting on the deck at the Sedona Rouge Hotel and Spa.

"That's why I wanted to bring you here," Simon smiled as he watched the glow on his son's face. "They have names for the formations. The one over there they call Snoopy because he looks like Snoopy lying on top of his doghouse. That one there is called Lucy. That one is Coffee Pot Rock. We'll get out later in the week so you can see Bell Rock, Cathedral Rock and Rabbit Ears."

"Why you know so much about this place, pops,"

"This is where I came after your moms left me. My former therapist told me there was a magnetic force in these formations. Some believe it's because of the Native American burial ground nearby. I needed a place to heal my spirit, so I came here."

"So, why did you bring me here?"

"I wanted to share with you a place that helped me get through it all. Sometimes you need to get away from things and find a place to reconnect with your spirit. I wanted to give you something I wished I had gotten long ago."

"What did you get, pops?"

"Look at that sunset, son. God made that for us. Look at those formations. It's all a reminder that there is so much more to life than what we see in the city. We can get so lost in doing for the sake of building more so we can get more that we forget the simple things in life. The best things in life are found in God's creation."

"I get that, pops."

"Creation has a way of reminding you of why you are you. When I came here I was so hurt because I felt like I let you and Carmen down. I was scared because at the same time your moms left me, I was leaving Shady Grove. That was a lot to carry at one time. It felt like the world was spinning out of control and I couldn't stop it. I needed a place to be still. A place to listen to God and find my inner self."

"It seems like you knew what I needed," Chris began to cry again. His life seemed chaotic. Instead of feeling great about going off to college, he felt guilt for impregnating Cheryl.

"We can thank God for that, Chris. But there is something in these rocks that is speaking to you,"

"What's that, pops? That I fucked up my life?"

"No, that you are man enough to work through whatever life brings. Having a baby doesn't end things for you, Chris. It only shifts things a bit. In the end your life will be more rich because of it all. Whatever Cheryl decides to do, you will be able to work through it, and you will look back on this day and thank God for sitting here to reflect on all it means."

"I wish it were that easy."

"Didn't say it was easy. I said you have what it takes inside to work through it all. Would you like to know what I was thinking when I sat in this same chair?"

"Sure, pops."

"I thought of the day you were born. I remembered how scared I was when your moms told me she was pregnant. I was scared because I had plans that didn't include having a baby. I didn't want to get married, but I did because I wanted to be there for my son. I sat here and wondered if I did the right thing. God spoke to me then."

"What did God say, pops?"

"That love was there for me in whatever decision I made. If I hadn't gotten married love would have been there for me. Then I questioned how love was present given the loss of the marriage. I sat here and cried my eyes out because I would not be there for you. Already I was hurting because I wanted my son and daughter near me, and they were being taken away. A part of me was lost and I couldn't do anything to stop it."

"I know, pops."

"I knew that I wouldn't have changed anything to be close to my children. I knew it wasn't a mistake to marry your mother because it gave me the chance to be the father I have been. I knew that I have made my share of mistakes over the years, but loving you was not one of them."

"You saying I should marry Cheryl."

"No, son. You're not ready to get married. What you are ready for is being a good father. If Cheryl decides to keep this baby you have everything inside of you to be the pops you need to be. There's a secret to parenting that folks don't tell you. God gives you what you need when you need it. It's all inside of you."

"I don't know what to do, pops."

"Be you, son. That's all you need to do. Be you and do what you've done to get you to this place. God will carry you through. I have a promise for you."

"What, pops?"

"I'll be there for you. I will help you through it all. You don't have to carry this on your own. Have you told your moms?"

"Nope."

"Who have you told?"

"Carmen."

"What did she tell you?"

"She told me to call pops because he would know what to say to help me through it all," Simon began crying now. He tried the best he could to hold back the tears, but his children, both of them, came to him in this time of need.

"Don't you go crying too, pops."

They both laughed. "Those are tears of joy, son."

"Ain't no joy in this."

"Yes there is. A bunch of joy. I'm so proud of both of you."

"Even though I fucked up?"

"Stop saying that, son. You didn't fuck up anything. Having a baby is a blessing from God, not a curse. I'm proud to be your father.

I'm proud to be Carmen's father. I'm proud at the bond the two of you have. And, I'm so thankful that we are sitting here having this talk. And I'm crying for one more reason."

What's that, pops?"

"That you didn't tell that asshole Maurice before you told me," laughter blended with tears as the sun concluded its setting over the red rocks of Sedona. "I have something to give you."

"What you got?" Simon reached under his chair where a box had been placed. In the box was a handmaid journal. The soft Italian calfskin cover closed with leather ties. The faint-lined buttery cream pages made it clear that this wasn't a normal journal purchased at a local bookstore.

"I had a friend of mine make this for you. I told him this was your first journal and I wanted it to be special. That my son was a man of class and needed to begin his journaling process in a classy journal."

"Dang!"

"We have six more days here. This is what I want you to do. I want you to get up every morning with the rise of the sun to write in this journal. Write whatever is on your mind. I want you to come back just before the sun sets to do the same thing. You don't have to share what you write with anyone. It's between you and God. I'm going to sit over there and do the same thing."

"I can dig that. Thanks, pops. "

The next six days was one adventure after another. They went to the Sedona Art Center where Simon purchased a painting for Chris. Chris fell in love with "Red Rock Crossing Autumn Color" painted by local artist Janet Noll Naumen. Chris was shocked when it was in his room when he returned. Simon also purchased an ocean jasper and sterling cabochon bracelet created by local artist Nancy Biher. It was Carmen's gift.

Chris spent two days in a spiritual retreat at SpiritQuest. They went horseback riding, took a balloon tour and rode the Sedona Trolley highlighting the Chapel of Holy Cross and The Sedona Seven Canyons. They enjoyed live jazz at the Rouge Hotel, got massages and ate like kings. The feature of everyday was the same

– sunrise and sunset on the patio of the Rouge. There, as the sun rose in the morning and set in the evening, they both rested in quiet reflection as words made way to pages.

Six days of spiritual healing was what both Simon and Chris needed. Father was there for his son in a time of need. Without knowing it, son was there for father to help quiet the old ghost ready to capture the last piece of joy remaining. Pops needed his son's love, and son needed his Pops's guidance. In six days they became more than father and son, they became best friends.

Chris left with a confidence. He was ready to go play ball and study hard. Simon was ready to lead the church again. Both would return to challenges, but they had the memory of seven days to carry them through the chaos waiting. More than that, they had each other to encourage the other after each step taken.

JUNE
Beauty • Humility

No person is your friend who demands your silence,
or denies your right to grow
-Alice Walker-

THE RETURN TO DURHAM SNAPPED Simon back into reality. The brief escape to the red rocks of Sedona rekindled Simon's passion for life again. The fleeting oasis away from the clamor in the news and the demands of the work reminded Simon of why he needed time away from the work. The phone rang within seconds of his closing the door. He ran to place his bags next to his bedroom door and reached for the phone.

"Pastor, this Kevin. Me and Peaches bout to be evicted and..." Simon listened as the crack-addicted partner of The Light House shared his sad story. Simon made a few calls to set things in motion to help Kevin pull his life back together after the most recent relapse.

The mountaintop experience of Sedona was followed by the valley of Durham. The work in the valley can numb the spirit, if you let it. Simon's retreat away gave him the strength to keep lingering in the work. Reconnecting with his son encouraged him. He could not help but think that part of what helped Chris cope with his own battles was witnessing how his father had served people in the church. Chris and Carmen had developed skills by watching Simon encounter a variety of circumstances.

The day was filled with normal church business. It was the business of helping people with real problems. The move to the school limited Simon's access to people. They called him at home now, and there was no office to meet. He refused to allow the lack of a facility to curtail the work. He kept reminding himself that Jesus didn't have an office. Jesus moved from place to place.

Simon drove down Hwy 55 to meet one of the partners about problems in his marriage. He checked the time on the dashboard – 2:30 p.m. He had an hour before they were scheduled to meet. He could feel the stress of jetlag and a busy day warring with his body. He needed coffee and could use the time to check his email.

He parked in a space in front of the Ideas Coffee House. Simon grabbed his laptop from the trunk and went inside. "What's up, Reverend Dr. Pastor?" D. J. Kraze, one of the owners joked as he walked in. "What did we do today to deserve your most holy presence?"

"Can't a brother just come to get some coffee without being harassed by a black man," Simon joked back. "Can't we all just get along?"

"Here comes one of them dignified Negroes," Dr. Ashanti, a professor of African Culture and Religion at North Carolina State University added. "Let us bow for the important Negro in the house."

They laughed as they continued the familiar game of teasing each black man who walked in the shop. It was part of the rites of passage that made Ideas Coffee House a special place for black men.

The Imperial Barber Shop provided that same feel – a healing station for black men – places to celebrate other black men working hard to pass on lessons to their sons and daughters. "Just give me a white chocolate mocha before I come back there and teach you who the boss is."

"Whew, the preacher just lost his religion, Kraze," Dr. Ashanti laughed.

"I'll help him find Jesus again if he steps back here," Kraze snapped back.

"I'm selling tickets. Who got $10 bucks for the show," Dr. Ashanti bantered as Simon opened his laptop. "Everyone be quiet. We got a lady coming in the house."

"Afternoon," Kraze greeted his female customer with class. "Can I help you?"

"That's his way of saying you fine as hell and can he get your number," Darrick inserted causing an eruption of laughter.

"Hey, Simon," Simon's head rose from his table as she called his name. It was Bonita.

"Damn! I'm getting me a license to preach. Them preachers get all the fine women. Between the women and the chicken I can't get nothing," Kraze screamed as she walked toward his table.

"Why haven't you called me?"

"Cause he's a damn fool," Ashanti answered. "Give me your number and I'll call."

"Don't mind them. They're not used to being in the presence of a queen," Simon rose from his table and embraced his old friend. I should have called. I don't have an excuse."

"Fool, fool, fool," Ashanti continued.

"Let me introduce you to these fools," Simon knew the game wouldn't end until he made formal introductions. "That bald headed sucker over there is D.J. Kraze. He owns this place with his father and uncle. That man over there with the big earrings and dashiki is Dr. Ashanti, our local scholar of all things from the motherland. And that big Negro over there is Darrick, aka 'the phone man'. Everyone, this is my good friend Bonita and yes I know she's fine."

"Welcome to Ideas, Bonita," Kraze said. "Your drink is on the house today. Least I can do since we bothered you so bad. Today it's on me. After today it's on that fool who didn't call you." They laughed some more. She ordered cherry Italian soda. They took a seat on the couch away to get some privacy.

"So, I hear things are good at The Light House," it was time for updates. Simon didn't know where to begin.

"The truth is things are falling apart. It's been a tough time."

"I'm sorry to hear that. You are so gifted."

"I thought you might have been through by now. Why haven't you come to see me?"

"Probably for the same reason you haven't called me, Simon. We both know there were rumors. Everywhere we go and every time people see us together they assume we are together. Look at them looking at us over there." She was right. They were watching.

'That's funny. I don't care about them. They'll tease me about you later. I can't say that I blame them."

"Why is that?"

"Because you are fine as hell."

"That's the first time you have ever made a comment about the way I look."

"Just because I never said it doesn't mean I didn't think it."

"So, why haven't you said it?"

"Because I didn't want to overstep the boundaries of our friendship."

"So telling me you are attracted to me is stepping over a boundary?"

"It could?"

'How is that, Simon?"

"It could lead to something else if we start talking like that."

'So you're scared that if you tell me you're attracted to me it might lead to more than a friendship?"

"Something like that."

"That's funny."

"Why is it funny?"

"It's funny because of the way you have been fooling yourself for all these years."

"What do you mean?"

"Simon, we have always had more than just a friendship. What we have is much deeper than that. The problem is we both have enough control not to go there. We both know we are attracted to each other and we both know we have feelings that are so much deeper than what we can say."

"Why you telling me this now, Bonita? If it's how you felt why didn't you just say that before?"

"Because I didn't know how I really felt until you left to go to Dallas with Jamaica. I remember the conversation we had before you left. You called me, happy about leaving. We talked about how you struggled all week with your decision to leave the church. I prayed hard for you to be free. I cried so much for you, Simon. I thought it was because you were a good friend and that's all it was between us. Then you left to be with her and it hurt me. It hurt because we had such a good thing and neither of us was strong enough to tell the truth."

"You still could have told me how you felt, Bonita."

"No, I couldn't. Not after how Sophie threw herself on you after thinking you would be her husband. Do you remember the conversation we had about how crazy you thought she was for reading stuff into the relationship that wasn't there? Think about it. Why wouldn't I think that you would feel the same way about me? There is no way in the world that I would put myself out there like that. If you have feelings I needed to hear you say it first."

"You been staying away from me because of all of this?"

"No, I've been staying away from you because you haven't cared enough about me. You pushed me away. As soon as someone else filled your space you pushed me to the curve. I gave up on being there because you found Patsy to take care of you instead of me," Simon was shocked to hear her call Patsy's name.

"How did you know about Patsy?"

"Everybody knows about Patsy. You think you are keeping it secret? This is Durham, Simon. People talk and people see things. You can't hide shit in Durham."

"Wow. I don't know what to say."

"All I can say is be careful, Simon. Not everyone who appears to be in your corner is in your corner. Just be careful."

"What does that mean?"

"It means be careful. That's all I have to say about that. Okay?"

"Sounds like the boys were right about me."

"What you talking bout, Simon?"

"I am a damn fool," he smiled at her. "You have been incredible, Bonita. I wouldn't have made it through none of that stuff without you. I have missed you. The truth is I have stayed away because I didn't want them to be right. With all those rumors about us I didn't want them to say I told you so."

"Simon. Oh boy," she sighed. "I get it. I understand you so much it hurts sometimes. I'm not sure if I would have done things different if I were in your shoes. It had to be hard going through all of that, and I do remember all of our conversations. I know things no one else knows."

"That's true."

'I know about how you were sexually abused as a child. I know about your struggles with drugs. Simon, I know it all. That's what makes us friends. We are truly friends. You know as much about me. You know about my being abused as a child. You helped me through my addiction. You know about my short-term relationship with a woman. You know so much about me, but you have never judged me, Simon. You cared for me in all I have gone through."

"I see what you're saying."

"We care about each other because of what we have carried together. We have never kissed. We never made love. What we have is pure and special and it would hurt both of us to be put in a place where it was thought of in a bad way. I understand, Simon. I just owe it to myself to tell you the truth. I promised myself that I would tell you when you made a statement like the one you did. When you said "you fine," that opened the door for me. Now you need to know the truth, Simon. Simon, I love you," she didn't care that others were listening.

"Don't say a word, Simon. Don't say I love you too. Just take it in. Let it soak. Go back and consider each conversation we have had. Think long and hard before you say a word. If you love me it will come natural. Not because you feel obligated to say it because of what I said. Say it because it consumes you."

Kraze and Ashanti were nodding their heads. They knew Simon's story and loved him like a brother. They wanted what was best for him and felt the passion of a beautiful woman who had just said I love you.

"One more thing, Simon. I'm glad I said it here before these men of good taste. I'm not afraid to let the world know how I feel, and I trust that these brothers will support us in whatever we do. No matter what, you have my friendship. If you want it, you have my love." She walked out the door with her Italian Soda in her hand. Dr. Ashanti clapped as she walked out the door. Kraze and Darrick joined his applause.

"Rev, please invite me to the wedding," Ashanti said as he placed his arm around his friend. "That there is a classy woman."

"Amen to that," Darrick added. 'Let the whole damn church say Amen."

It had been a while since Simon had been to the beach. Pasty was thrilled to get away to be free and spending time with Simon without any restrictions. They both needed time away from phone calls and other interruptions. They also needed time to reconnect after Simon's trip to Chicago and Sedona. It seemed like months since they had been together. Her new work kept her on the road. That, combined with his time away, was the cause of increasing tension between the two of them. They had not made love in more than a month. She could never find the time to be with him. Her new job in marketing with IBM kept getting in the way.

His phone rang as they passed the Wade Avenue exit headed East on HWY 40.

"That's my phone, baby," he warned her. "It may be the newspaper about my coming back to write a column." The number showed up private. He couldn't take the chance. He touched the receive button on his blue tooth.

"Handle your business, baby."

"This is Simon Edwards."

"Now I know how to get you to answer the phone," it was Jamaica.

"How you been," the change in tone caught Patsy's attention. It was obvious this wasn't about business.

"I've been fine. I'm busy right now."

"Too busy to talk to an old friend?"

"I'm with my girlfriend right now. I'm on my way to the beach."

"Oh, I see. Tell her your Jamaica says hello."

"I'll be sure to do that."

"Tell me one thing, Simon. Do you miss me?"

"Yes, but that doesn't matter. I really need to go."

"Why? Because you're gonna get in trouble because she knows you still want me?"

"I don't know the answer to that. I'm disrespecting her by having this conversation with you. So, I need to go."

"Will you call me later?"

"Why should I do that? Give me one reason?"

"Because I want you."

"Whatever. I have to go," Simon hung up the phone in rage. He did his best to hide the emotions, but Patsy noticed something was wrong with the phone call. He had no intention of hiding who was on the other line. "That was Jamaica."

"I kind of figured that. What the bitch want?"

"She wanted to talk and I told her it wasn't a good time."

"So, you plan to call her later?"

"Patsy, I have nothing to say to Jamaica."

"Have you two been talking before today?"

"No, that's the first time we have talked. She's called but I haven't answered the phone."

"I'm supposed to believe that?"

"It's the truth."

"You want me to believe of all the times she gets through, it's when I'm in the car. Seems to me like it would have been easy to get through."

"Today she blocked the id. I didn't know it was her calling. All the other times her number popped up."

"So, what did she say when you told her you were with me?"

"She wanted to know if I would get in trouble for talking to her."

"I bet she did ask that. She wants to know if you still want her. That bitch is trying to get you back."

"That may be true but all that matters is I'm with you and not with her. It should matter to you that I haven't talked to her when she calls me. If I was so into her I would be talking to her. I would be talking to her since you can't find time to be with me anymore."

"What is that supposed to mean?"

"It means what I said. You don't have time for us anymore. You have been so busy since I made the trip to Chicago. It's like you've been punishing me for not taking you with me. You're always out of town. Not to mention you don't answer your phone when I call you. What is that about?"

"It's about me trying to make a living. I can't help it if I get bad reception."

"Yeah, and you get bad reception wheRever you go. They must not have phones in those hotel rooms because the last I checked you can use those to say hello."

"Don't be mad at me because I have a life, Simon. I don't get pissed at you for having a life."

"I'm not upset, just making a point. You want to be upset with me because Jamaica calls. I don't have nothing to do with that. I have tried my best to make time with you. I'm trying to work through my issues and get to where you want me to be, but you keep pulling away from me. It's like I'm constantly having to deal with issues with you. Well, Jamaica is not an issue between us. That is my past and I'm trying to have a future with you."

"Answer this then, Simon. Do you still have feelings for her?"

"Of course I do. I have a bunch of them. I have anger. I have regret. I have disappointment. I've got feeling like a damn fool for letting her in my life. Is that enough? Want some more?"

"Do you still love her?"

"I do. You know that. What does that have to do with this? What does that have to do with us going to the beach to spend some time together? How many times do I have to have the conversation with you? I'm tired of talking about Jamaica," Simon's voice began to rise.

"Fine then. We don't have to talk about Miss Thang."

"Praise God for that! Since we're past that, there is one thing I need to ask you."

"What now?"

"You know people are talking about us now?"

"No, I didn't know that."

"Seems we're the talk of the city. It always amazes me that I'm the last one to know when I'm the news of the day."

"What do you mean by that?"

"When Janet was fucking Maurice everyone knew but me. Hell, it came up at the church business meeting. Now, we've been talking about your issues with me not sharing our relationship in public and it's already the talk of the town. Isn't that a trip? I'm getting grief for something that isn't a real problem. The thing that is tripping me out the most is that you knew it all along. In fact you may be the reason behind it becoming public."

"Wait a minute, Simon. Don't be blaming me for that."

"It's cool, Patsy. I'm not mad at you for it. You have a right to share what we have. I never gave you a gag order. The thing that bothers me is in how you walk around acting like it's so hard for you to be comfortable because you can't be free with what we have only to find out that you've been on blast about this from day one."

"Whatever, Simon."

"It all came to me when my friend Bonita mentioned our relationship."

"What that bitch have to say about me?" the name Bonita perked Patsy's attention. Simon knew it would.

"It's not nice to call your relative a bitch, Patsy. That's right. I know she's your cousin. Didn't take much to figure that out. People keep telling me Durham is a small town. I figured I would start acting like other people and ask some fucking questions. Since everyone wants to be in my business and all."

"So what you find out, Mr. Big Shot investigator?"

"I was told that you've been telling people you were going to get me for a long time. Before I left Durham. I heard that you have been open about our relationship and everyone is talking about it. That's cool with me because it hasn't become a problem. In a strange way all of this has proven to me that I can be free. No one is digging into my personal business this time. So, I suppose I should thank you for setting me free, Patsy. I'm not mad at you for it, but please do me a favor. Stop talking to me about what I'm not willing to do when it comes to the church. Since you already put us on blast I would like it very much if you stop using that as an excuse."

"Whatever, Simon!"

"Please, spare me the drama, Patsy. I will do that when I have the confidence in us to lead me to make that type of move. I'm still working on getting to know you. Yes I love you, but right now I'm not liking you very much. This trip might help with that. Let's just say there have been some changes that have me wondering about you. I've been through enough to know to listen to that inner voice. It may be God trying to tell me something. I'm not saying there is something wrong, but it smells like something is wrong."

"That's bullshit, Simon, and you know it."

"There is one thing I do know. Everyone I talked to told me to be careful. No one would say why. They said be careful. Makes you wonder, doesn't it?" he looked at Patsy in search for a reaction. Then he smiled. In the middle of his smile her phone vibrated. He noticed it light up in her hand. "That's your phone ringing. Don't you think you should get it?"

"That's okay. It can wait."

Forgiveness is one of those tricky things that everyone talks about without knowing what it means. Most people are lucky enough never to have to test the waters of forgiveness. It's not the same unless you have been stabbed in the back and left to bleed to death. Simon had been stabbed over and over again. Being back in Durham, having slid back to that place where he faced a spiritual execution, meant constantly facing those who stood on the other side of the lever.

They were everywhere. When they appeared they brought with them the fake smiles and the phony greeting: "how you doing Pastor?" Some claimed they loved him. Others wanted the dirt to take back to those waiting for proof of his deviant disposition. Simon learned to smile, shake hands, give an occasional hug and to move on as if none of it mattered.

He wanted to believe it was all for the better. It wasn't. Not getting paid wasn't better. The loss of a vital ministry wasn't better. It wasn't better to watch another minister reap the benefits of his hard work. Facing walking away was harder than he imagined when he said yes to the light calling him to come back to Durham. Coming back forced a constant inner inventory. It meant persistent spiritual overhaul. Each day meant the possibility of yet another encounter with that mean past.

The hardest part was in dealing with the callous nature of his critics. None of them seemed to recognize the sin of their ways. They functioned as if God was in command of their actions. They easily pitted themselves against Simon and what they regarded as his evil ideology, and praised the Most High for helping them win the battle. This was a war of theological perceptions – the conservative mindset versus the progressive conceptions found over at The Light House.

Simon reviled their oppressive ways. Their smiles denoted the smallness of their thinking. They measured God's work by numbers and programs. They flaunted the confirmation of their positions by using membership size, budget, the bulk and beauty of the church buildings and the compensation of their pastor. All Simon had to offer was the message and his faith. As he witnessed to those motivated by external confirmation, he noticed a strange transformation in the way he thought about the work of the kingdom. Something was happening to him. He was changing for the better.

The first step was forgiveness. He would never be free until he learned how to forgive. The movement toward authentic forgiveness mandated learning to love self first. Simon was learning to do that void of regret. With each passing month, a part was released. The spirit of deception had worked overtime to rob Simon of his true identity. Month by month, day by day, a part of his violated spirit was being restored. Deception claimed he was a bad father. Simon learned that was not true. Deception challenged him to see failure in his work and life. Simon was beginning to understand what it meant to be free.

Freedom can never place life in small boxes. Oppression is the upshot of compartmentalizing life. There's a box for relationships. Another box for parenthood and another for the work one does. Those boxes lead to a fragmented life – one minimized by refusing to embrace what it means to be a whole person. Simon was learning to walk in his new freedom. It was beginning to feel good. It fit him well because it was his life that he was wearing now, not the life enthused by the expectations of the people who tried to keep him in those boxes.

His newfound freedom brought new challenges, like how to make it all fit in one open box. He was learning to fit everything within the same life rather than creating different lives for different situations. Simon was tired of the chameleon existence that regulates the working of the church. Nothing is real. It is a game designed to fool all who participate. They come with their fake smiles and rehearsed Hallelujah's. They come with their false claims of holiness and pointed fingers. They play the church game on Sundays and go back to being liars and cheaters the very next day. Simon was learning the worth of openness and the power of authentic freedom. You can't be free until you learn to forgive.

Forgiveness has a way of finding you. It forces you to deal with its need. You can't keep it to yourself. It has to be shared. Forgiving words must be spoken. More than that, they must be felt when spoken. You can't hide true forgiveness. It knows when it comes from the heart. The need for forgiveness will find you. It needs the release from the bondage that you hold in your possession. It cries out, please set me free, tell me you forgive me; let me know that I no longer have to hold the guilt of what I did to you.

Forgiveness followed Simon to The Light House. It sat on the third row one Sunday morning. He noticed forgiveness in the middle of the first prayer. It was the prayer to evoke God's presence. In the prayer he spoke of the significance of gathering. "We come together to express our communal faith," he prayed. "And in our gathering, we become the vessels of your Spirit. We are the power of your love, peace and forgiveness..." He saw forgiveness there. In the middle of that word – forgiveness – he saw Sophie sitting in tears.

His first thought was Judas. She had betrayed Simon for $10,000. She told lies for a cash payment. It didn't matter. The people loved him enough to not listen to those fabrications. They saw through her obsession over the Preacha' Man. They knew her desire for him, and how bad things get when a woman is scorned. Their refusal to buy in to those lies did not cover the pain of their intent. Simon saw his Judas sitting in the third row.

Forgiveness met him on his own turf. It forced him to contend with his own words. "Forgive those who despitefully use you," those holy words. "Turn the other cheek" those words deemed fundamental to the teachings of his faith now met him and forced him to respond. They became more than a message of a Sunday teaching moment. He was forced to embrace the image of himself posted on that cross he claimed to carry, and to cry out "forgive her, for she knows not what she does."

He saw her crying, and those tears transformed his hatred. He knew those tears. They reminded him of that weekend before he stood before the church to announce he could take no more. He remembered the grapple of his soul - like Isaac wrestling with himself before God changed his name. He remembered cuddling and crying, aching and pleading to find rest from the pain. He saw that same look on Sophie's face. It forced him to change his prayer.

"God, we see the broken here today. They are broken by the life they have chosen. Broken by the things they have said, by the things they did not say. Broken by the things they have done to bring harm to those they love," he felt the Spirit lifting him in the moment of his offer of forgiveness.

"God, this brokenness must end today. The time has come to shatter its rule and announce its death. Die, pain. You have no home here. Die, shame. There is no room for you in this vessel that belongs to you. Die, humiliation. She, yes I said she, has stepped into this holy place to find her peace again," the congregation erupted into one of those rare spiritual moments. It was clear to all that this time was set for Sophie's healing.

"Set Sophie free. Set Sophie free," Sophie's tears overwhelmed her as the partners gathered to console her. "Show her there is no bitterness in this room. Show her we walk in the Spirit of the one who set us free to love and forgive. Teach her that her life is renewed and your forgiveness forces my forgiveness. Teach her that all of us are free to love again. There is no bitterness. There is no separation."

Sophie fell to her knees too ashamed to look up. She couldn't stop the tears. The love of the church would lift her. Simon felt a release that had him crying too. He knew, in that moment, that he too was free from the pain of his past experience. In forgiving Sophie he received the power of his own forgiveness. The church knew it. They celebrated what they had witnessed in their leader. More than words spoken, they were eyewitnesses to faith in action. More than words spoken, they witnessed love in their midst.

The congregation loved her to her healing. They became bearers of the light. The Light House was that light she needed. One by one they embraced her. Over and over again she heard them say "We love you, Sophie." Each of them meant it. Their light forced them to love. The words spoken, week after week, had formed true faith. Simon was witnessing the emergence of the ministry he had prayed for. Before his eyes he saw love in action.

He waited his turn before going to her. That sweet Spirit within him beckoned him to wait for the others to say I love you. His turn came after the last embrace. He stood behind her. "Sophie," he called her name. "I love you. Christ loves you. Be free, Sophie. Just be free and let the love of God guide you." He grabbed hold of her and hugged her tight. He held her in the way she had wished. She wanted to feel his embrace, but this was not an unholy moment with thoughts of lust. This was sacred space where guilt meets love, and love overcomes shame.

"I love you too, Pastor," the stuttered words were met with more sobs. "I am so...."

"Shh, don't say a word, Sophie. I know you're sorry. Just receive this love and be free. Hear me. Be free," she nodded her head as the choir sang. They sang and sang and sang and hugged each other and shared the love. Each was filled with joy because they were at The Light House. They sang and sang and sang.

"This little light of mine, I'm gonna let it shine."

JULY

Love • Security • Jealousy

Holding on to anger is like grasping a hot coal with the intent of throwing it at someone else; you are the one who gets burned.
-Buddha-

IN DEATH THERE IS LIFE. That's the meaning of resurrection. Old things wither to make room for rebirth. Something has to die before something can live. Simon felt something dying. With the death of his former self, came the emergence of a new Simon. He felt the change. Loss didn't mean the same anymore. He walked with a new confidence. At first, Simon feared change. It creeps up on you when you least expect it. You can't force change. It comes with the change in season – naturally. It is part of God's way of recreating things in need of help.

The change came in the middle of confusion – confusion forced by those around him. Their issues swarmed his space in hope of dominating his peace. It didn't this time. Before he would have taken a back seat in order to fix the pains of those around him but now, for the first time, he clinched his limits. He no longer feared the limits of his life. He knew, for the first time, his place in the universe. He could no longer play God. He could no longer take the blame for the actions of other people.

Change has a way of impacting the people around you. Some envy your peace. Others become confused by the radical shift. It forces a readjustment in the way they attack. Their need to render others stripped of self-worth is overpowered when one refuses to play the game. Simon was learning to be comfortable in his own skin. Freedom was coming, little by little, as God taught those tough lessons.

Simon checked the balance in his savings account. Less than $2,000 remained, and his only source of income was from writing a column for the *Herald-Sun*. The $250 a week he made kept him afloat. He was at peace with things. The number did not sway him. He still believed in the work but, more than that, he was not looking for the work to pave the way for economic security.

He waited for Calvin while sipping his coffee at the Blue Coffee Café. He pressed *send* to submit his weekly column. He wrote in response to three crosses burning in the city on the same night. "Given we have created an environment where lunatics believed it was appropriate to burn three crosses, let's commit to engage in ongoing conversations with a person who is different," He wrote. "Imagine people from across the city busy meeting, eating, and getting to know someone completely different. The commitment has to go beyond a one-time affair. You can't get to know a person after eating chicken one time. Spend considerable time together. Don't limit the conversation to just race. Have a conversation with a gay person or a person of a different faith."

He felt the merging of his two ministries – journalism and the church. He was finally free to write in a way that reflected his true passion. He no longer had to censor himself out of fear for how the leadership at Shady Grove would respond. They had demanded that he stop writing. They felt his writing gave the church a bad name in the community. He refused to write what they wanted, and he would not recant those words to appease them. Simon was free to write, and the comforts that came with that meant more to him than a big paycheck.

"Are you Simon Edwards?" a customer at the coffee house asked.

'I am."

"I love your column. Durham needs your voice. Keep up the good work," the white man in his mid forties reached out his hand in an offer to shake. "I'm Bill Guthrie. I own a business over on Main

Street. I like what you had to say about economic development in the downtown district."

'Thanks for that. It always helps knowing how my readers feel about what I write."

"Yeah, I have been reading your columns for years. I hated it when you left town. It's good to have you back in the paper."

"Hey Rev, that was a good piece," Cliff, a regular at the coffee house added. "People need to celebrate the good things that are happening in Durham instead of always tearing us down."

"Just be sure to let the new owners know how you feel," Simon asked. "You know they're making wholesale changes at the paper." Simon was concerned that the new owners would terminate him in an effort to save money. Already a number of the established writers had been let go.

"My Pastor," Calvin entered the room and greeted Simon with a hug. "You keeping in trouble," they both laughed at the assertion.

"You know I love trouble." Simon joked as Calvin ordered a cup of coffee and a slice of red velvet cake. They moved to the room in the back and sat on the couch.

"Man, people still talking about what happened last month when Sophie came to the church," Calvin started the conversation.

"Yeah, that was a powerful moment. I think it kind of sums up where we are as a church right now."

"What you mean by that, Pastor?"

"All that love in the room," Calvin smiled in agreement. "I saw what I have been praying for all these years, Calvin. It was like in that moment God let me know that we are on the right track."

"I'm glad to hear you say that because I've been concerned about you."

"I know you have, Calvin, and I do appreciate that," Simon paused to collect his thoughts. "But this is the first time in all my years of ministry that I understand what it means to be called."

"Now that's deep."

"It is deep. I have this peace about me that I never had before, Calvin. I wouldn't trade this feeling for anything."

"What do you mean when you say you understand the call? I'm asking because you know I'm considering ministry," Simon smiled when Calvin made that statement. He saw so much of himself in Calvin. He knew no one better equipped to take on the challenge of ministry.

"For all those years, Calvin, I did the work of ministry thinking I understood what it meant. I gave myself to being the best I could at it. I got the M.Div and Ph.D to get the knowledge I needed to lead God's folks. I did all of that, but still didn't understand the call like I do today."

"I hear you, Pastor."

"In all the humility that I prayed to bring to the work, deep down I had an expectation that it would reap certain benefits. I did it all for the perks. It became more of a vocation than a calling. I enjoyed all that came with standing in that hallowed place. I reaped the big salary, benefit package, housing allowance. I got all of that. I also got to be on the Revival tour where I would make $2,000 plus each week to preach the Word."

"I'm listening, Pastor."

"I became a part of that group of sacred superstar preachers called in to preach folks into a frenzy once a year. I played that game of feeding them emotions so that they would keep coming back each week to pour their hard earned money into that collection plate. I sold them the hope of a better life that could be theirs if they paid the price of becoming slaves to the institution we call the church."

'That's heavy, Pastor. I feel you."

"I was one of the boys of the trade. The big cats would call me in. They called to check in on me in hope that I would have them come in for my once a year Revival. I would go to the big conferences and meet more big shot preachers. I would hear them preach and would leave impressed at their oratory skills. I would leave thinking I needed to have that one come over to my place to get the folks happy.

"I played that game. I dressed the part of the big time Preacha' Man. I would go to New York to get my suits made by the best and have shirts tailored made with my initials on my sleeves. I would buy those expensive shoes with the designer names and flaunt my Cartier watch. I played that game, Calvin. I played it well, all in the name of Jesus."

"So what's different now, Pastor?"

"Something bothered me, Calvin. I noticed that all of those friends who used to call me stopped calling. All of the people who stepped in the pulpit where I once led no longer saw me as a person they needed to maintain contact with. I became a liability. They could no longer use me to promote their own agenda. I was old news. The leader of a small church now. Get this, Calvin; they stayed around long enough to see what would happen. They wanted to know if the work would blossom into mega status. Once it didn't happen they disappeared. They stopped returning my phone calls. They no longer checked up on me to see if everything was okay."

'That's cold, Pastor," Calvin felt pain for what his friend and Pastor had endured. Simon laughed.

"Don't get it twisted, Calvin. It's not a bad thing. A part of me had to die for me to live. Like them, I had been suckered into the lifestyle of ministry. God didn't call me to become a part of the sacred boys' and girls' holy society. This work isn't about what I get out of it. This work is about the people who need something real. God is not calling us to build great businesses, Calvin. God is calling us to build lives."

"That's what you saw with Sophie?"

"God taught me a lesson that day, Calvin. You see, I was still holding on to things that I had to let go of in order to move forward. I can't let the actions of others impact my movement in the Spirit. I can't let the pain of loss and rejection hinder my thoughts around who I am in ministry. There's one more thing, Calvin."

"What, Pastor?"

"You have to understand, the entire church needs to know I'm at peace with being here. Some of you may feel guilty due to how things have not worked out in the way we wanted. Like the rest of you I want to be able to look in my bank account and see more than enough. I want those things, Calvin. I would lie if I said I didn't. But I have learned what rich life looks like. I'm free to love the Lord and do this work not for what I get out of it but because I'm called to do it. There is no salary attached to a call, Calvin."

"We want to do more for you, Pastor."

"I know you do. I know you love me. I also know you feel guilty for begging me to come back to Durham. Am I wrong?"

"No, it's been eating at me real bad."

"Calvin, look at me when I say this. Look at me, Calvin! I thank God for being here. I'm at peace. I may not have the things I have become accustomed to, but I am at peace. This is where God wants me. Thank God for my peace, Calvin. The rest will come in time."

They ended the conversation with talk about Calvin's call to ministry. Calvin left strengthened by the discussion and more focused on what it means to do the work of ministry.

"Look, Jamaica, I don't want to have a conversation about the good old days," Simon had held off answering her calls as long as he could. He needed time to process his feelings. It was time to say what needed to be said.

"You trying to tell me that you've got all of me out of your system?" her seductive flare came through the phone with hopes of finding Simon's weak spot.

"I'm telling you that I am over you. What I felt before is over and I have no reason to come see you."

"I'm supposed to believe that? Is that your Holy Roller side talking, or did your new girlfriend force you to say that?"

"This has nothing to do with Patsy. This is about where I am and what I need in my life. There was a time when I would have enjoyed coming down there and making love to you. That time is over for me. I'm at a new place where I no longer want to play games with my life."

"You trying to say I'm just a game?"

"I didn't say that, Jamaica. I said I'm tired of playing games with my life. I'm looking for something different now. I need more than good sex to sustain my life. I'm too old for those old games."

"What we had was deeper than just sex, Simon. Both of us know that."

"That's true, Jamaica, but if I come down there now it would be just about sex. You have your man. I have my woman. What else would it be other than both of us playing games and cheating on the person in our life?"

"Maybe it would be about seeing if we have reason to get back together," Simon was shocked by that statement. "Maybe I'm willing to bend a bit on some things."

"Like what, Jamaica?"

'Like maybe I could move to Durham."

"Wow, can't believe I heard that," Simon thought about her offer for a few seconds. "So, what's really up, Jamaica? Having problems in negotiating your new contract?"

"Maybe. Does it matter? Isn't it enough that I would consider Durham as an option?"

"It would matter to me if it were an option before you had no option there. It's simple when it comes to what I need, Jamaica. I need a woman who will give the same thing I'm willing to give in a relationship. I need for her to make me a priority. I need for her to love everything about me. That means loving my work. That means loving and supporting my children. That means being there for me in every way, not just in bed."

"Simon, I'm willing to try."

"You shouldn't have to try. It should come natural. That isn't a criticism of you, Jamaica; it is a statement about what I need in my life. I need a woman who understands what I do and who can support me when I'm on the bottom. Right now things aren't going good with me here. Would you be able to stand being with a man who isn't Mr. It for today? Hmm. Can you deal with the Simon who no longer is the big baller?"

"Damn, Simon, you talk like I ain't never seen bad times in my life! You forget I'm from the fucking hood! You forget how I struggled to get where I am today! I haven't always lived on lobster and steak! I know what it means to support a person when they're down! I've been down and have needed that in my own life!" Simon had to pause as he listened to Jamaica pour her heart out. For the first time, he believed her. He believed she was willing to give it a try.

"That's easy to say, Jamaica. Being with me while I do my work isn't easy."

"Fuck that shit. I've told you that from day one when I refused to be a part of it all. I didn't want it when you were Mr. Big Shit Preacha Man. I didn't want it when your black ass was on the cover of magazines and shit. I didn't want it because I thought that shit through and knew I wasn't ready for all of that. You don't get this, Simon. This bitch is changing and it is scaring the Hell out of me."

"Why you scared?"

"Because Ms. Composed ain't in control no more!"

"What do you mean?"

"You wanna know! You really wanna know! Because the motherfucker I was seeing turned out to be married with damn kids. That asshole had a wife and I didn't know it. Turns out his wife finds out and calls the station. The station calls me and lets me go because they didn't want the bad press that she was threatening them with. She was ready to call the newspaper. She has pictures and shit from a private eye she hired to check in on that motherfucker."

"I'm sorry to hear all of that, Jamaica. I'm really sorry."

"So get this, Simon. How am I supposed to feel after letting a good man go for that lying son of a bitch? That's when it hit me. I should have come with you when I had a chance. Now that I've lost all of this what did I do it for? Huh! I was walking around like I'm all of that and all it took was a call, just like you said when you told me you were leaving, Simon. That's all it took to push my fine ass out the door."

"I know it hurts, baby. Everything will work out. You can trust that."

"Yeah, yeah, yeah. Your Jesus will work it out. Is that what you're telling me?"

"I'm telling you that you have too much talent to remain on the bottom. In the end this could be the thing you needed."

"I wish I could believe that, Simon. I just left the fucking station before calling you. I didn't know who else to call. I didn't want to call my mama. I don't want to worry her. I didn't know who to call. Simon, you are the only person I know who would listen and understand. I just need you right now," she broke into tears as she placed the phone away from her ear.

"Jamaica, Jamaica, Jamaica!"

"I'm here."

"Listen to me. Are you listening?"

"Yes."

"I need for you to know that things will work out for you. Do you believe that?"

"I'm sorry, Simon. I'm so sorry I fucked things up between us. I'm so, so sorry!"

"That doesn't matter now. You hear me. None of that matters. I need for you to understand that things will get better. Do you believe that?"

"I wish I could, Simon. Right now I don't know what to think."

"Can you do me a favor?"

"What is it?"

"I need for you to call me every day for the next month. Can you do that?"

"What will your woman think?"

"This is not about her. This is about your need for a friend. If she doesn't understand that then she is not the woman for me. Do you get that?"

"Thanks, Simon. I really need you now."

"I know you need a friend. I'll be that for you, Jamaica. There's one more thing."

"What, Simon?"

"I lied to you. I do still love you," you could hear the smile. "It's hard not to love you when you show your real side."

"I know you love me, Simon. I know."

"I'm telling you that because I want you to know I care for you. I'll be there for you, Jamaica. Just try to find the faith to hold on. This too will pass."

"Thanks, Simon. Thanks so much."

"Call me tomorrow."

"I will."

Simon decided to take a trip to Northwestern to see Chris play in a scrimmage. This time he asked Patsy to come. She couldn't make it due to a business trip. He called to tell her he made it to the campus, but, after the third call, she did not answer. He left a brief message and placed his cell phone back in its case.

"I'm glad you could make it, pops," Carmen said as she kissed Simon on the cheek. "For this awesome bracelet," she showed off the one he purchased in Sedona. "And for being such a good pops."

"Thanks, sweet sugar baby."

"I mean it, pops," she became serious as she spoke. "You really helped Chris with that trip. He hasn't been the same since he got back."

"It changed me too, baby. I don't think I will ever be the same again," the trip had transformed Simon. As much as he had planned it to help Chris prepare for the next stage of his life, it helped him press through some of the issues that had limited his perspective.

"Would you like to go with me in May of next year?" he had already planned for the trip. It seemed like the right time to ask.

"What! You kidding me? Oh my God. Oh my God. I want to go so bad!"

"The trip is already paid for," he smiled. "We leave the day after school ends. I already cleared it with your moms."

"Mom! You knew!" Carmen jumped from the bleachers to where her mother sat and hugged her tight. I love you too, mom. She uncovered the blanket from her newborn brother and kissed his forehead. "I love you too, Cecil."

She returned to Simon's side and gave him another kiss. "I love you, pops. Go, Chris, go, go, go, go."

Everyone rose to their feet as Chris ran for a 65 yard touchdown. "That boy is amazing," a fan behind them said. "He needs to be starting."

"That's my son," Simon said after turning his head to view the fan. "We hope you're right."

"I'm sure I am, Mister. My boy is number 46. He's a middle linebacker. Troy Burton his name. I'm William Burton. They call me Big Willie."

"Hey Big Willie," the whole gang responded in unison.

"See, pops. That's because of you," Carmen placed her arm around Simon. "You got him ready for this."

"He did all the work Carmen."

"You and the Big Dude upstairs worked on this one big time, pops," her face said it all. She was thankful for what Simon had done. "My big brother needed you and you came through like I knew you would."

"Don't make me cry, baby," Simon fought back the tears. "I only wish I could do more for you guys."

Chris ended the game with 97 yards rushing and 35 yards receiving. He was named the game's MVP. He had gained 15 pounds of muscle since leaving Sedona and he looked much faster than before. He walked up to Simon at the end of the game to give him high fives.

"What you think, pops?"

"You bad, boy. You bad."

"Coach just told me I'm first team now. Got to go talk to a few reporters. We still doing dinner? I'm starved."

"Yeah, we'll wait for you."

Carmen and Chris picked the place to eat. They went to the Davis Street Fish Market. Simon loved the place. He ordered the Bib Mamou. He had a craving for crawfish. The dish came with crawfish, shrimp and scallops sautéed in a spicy tomato sauce and served over rice. Chris ordered the Davis Street Etoufee and Carmen had the Chesapeake Bay Crab Cakes.

"It's good to know my babies have an appreciation for good cooking," Simon joked as the food came to the table. "I was expecting to order a Cajun Chicken Sandwich Combo at Bojangles."

"Come on, pops," Chris laughed. "How we gonna do you like that knowing you're Chef Negro Lagasse."

The two made fun of their father's kitchen antics. "This my kitchen, get out until I say it's time to eat. You messing with my concentration. This here, I say, this here is a masterpiece in the making. Can you smell the masterpiece brewing in the oven? Smell what is waiting for you tonight. Smell it. Smell it, I say. Your taste buds will never be the same again," Chris mocked with a bad French accent.

It felt like old times only better. Better because Chris and Carmen had grown up. The years hadn't tainted their childhood memories of Simon in the kitchen preparing meals for them. He missed cooking for them.

"So how you been feeling, Chris," he raised the question that had been on his mind since leaving Durham. "You okay with everything?"

"Go ahead and tell him, Chris" little sister moved closer to her brother as she encouraged him to share the pain. "Tell him."

"Tell me what?"

"Cheryl decided not to have the baby, pops," Chris said.

"How does that make you feel, son?"

"Kind of strange. In one way I'm okay, but in another I feel like I have lost a part of me. It hurts that it wasn't my decision. You know, that baby was a part of me too, but I had no voice in it. That hurts, pop. I was ready to do the right thing," Simon's pride in his son swelled even more.

"You were ready to be a father, son?"

"Yeah, I was after we left Sedona, pops. I wanted with my son what we had. I could see how good it made you feel and I wanted to be able to be that with my son or daughter. It's strange. I was so scared until I started writing in that journal. Stuff came out of me that I didn't know was there. I started looking at me. I had to ask myself if I could do it,if I was ready to be a father. I knew I could do it because I had an example to follow. Pops."

'That's good, son, but I've made some mistakes."

"That's what helped me the most, pops. It's not the mistakes you make. It's what you do with the mistakes you make. Something you said helped me see that. When you go down the wrong road you still have to drive. I could do it because I don't have to be perfect and I have support to help me through. I was looking forward to coming to you for help. You know, sort of like male bonding stuff. It's what I need the most. A real man who will be there for me. My pops."

"Why didn't you tell me before I got here?" Simon asked.

"Because I wanted to say this face to face. I wanted my little sister with me because we have something to give you – no, we got two things to give you. The first is the meal is on us," they puffed out their chest proud to say that. "We got you, pops."

"Now that's alright!"

"We got something else, pops," Carmen said. "This is from both of us."

"Yeah, we prayed about this one," Chris said. Both looked for his reaction.

"You both prayed over this?"

"We pray together every night. We have since moms moved in with the Ass Mo," Carmen added. "Sorry for cussing. Chris said you wouldn't mind. We call Maurice the Ass Mo. Not to his face though. Anyhow, we pray together each night."

"Wow, that's encouraging to know," Simon was moved by it all.

"Somebody needs to pray in the house, pops," Chris showed his disgust. After we prayed we decided it was probably a good thing that Cheryl had the abortion. Otherwise I would have a child the same age as my brother. That ain't cool, pops."

"I'll give you that. The thought has crossed my mind."

"Back to our gift. Go ahead, Chris."

"We wanted to give you something you didn't need. We wanted to give you something you already have because it's in you. We decided to give you back what you gave us so that you'll know that we have it now," Chris said as he pulled out a Bible from the bag in his hand.

"We want you to preach out of this Bible, pops," Carmen continued. "When you do think about us because you have poured so much into us. Because of you this thing controls us. We are who we are because of you and we like who we have become."

"Ya'll gonna make me cry over my crawfish," they laughed some more. "I'm so proud of the two of you. I couldn't have asked for better children."

"We know," they said in unison.

Simon tried one last time to reach Patsy. There was no answer. He picked up the Bible given to him at dinner. He opened it to the first page to read the inscription one more time. *We are with you when you preach the Word. We are with you because you placed it in both of us. Your disciples, your children, your biggest fans, Chris and Carmen.*

He processed the happenings of the day. From the look on Carmen's face when she heard she was going to Sedona to Chris's touchdown, the conversation at dinner to the receipt of his gift. It had been a wonderful trip. He bowed for prayer and thanksgiving for the way he had been carried to this point.

"God, thank you for restoring my children in the midst of insane circumstances. You carried them when their mother and I were dealing with our own mess. It is your grace that has sustained them. Continue to provide for them. Thank you for their wisdom and strength. Thank you for forgiving me of my shortcomings and seeing the good in me despite all the wrong I have done. Amen."

The month had come and gone. In it he had witnessed many miracles. He reflected on Sophie's visit to the church and how the love of the partners overwhelmed her. He recognized the growth within his spirit due to his being open to loving and forgiving her when she came. "I have come a long way, Lord. I thank you for this journey." He recognized the peace that had overtaken him since his return from Sedona.

He reflected on his conversation with Jamaica about the loss of her job. Since then the two had developed a deeper friendship. For the first time he had with her a relationship that was deeply spiritual. He was learning things about her he never knew. She hid her brokenness well, and he was thankful for being in a place to share with her void of sex. The sex had interfered with true intimacy. She still wanted more with him, but Simon was content in remaining friends.

Then there was Patsy. Something strange was happening between the two of them. Simon knew there was more to the story than was being told. He refused to harp on the unknowns, but rather focused on the things he could control. What mattered was his doing the right thing. He could not control Patsy; he could only love her, even when she wasn't available to receive his love.

He considered Bonita's love for him and a proper response. He fought the temptation to go to her to begin something new, something fresh and more fulfilling than anything he had experienced before. He knew that his newfound spirituality would help in building a significant relationship. He would never love in the same way again. No longer could he limit love to some physical force. Simon needed to bond to a woman's spirit. He could feel the power of that possibility.

The possibility was there with Bonita, but first there was unresolved business. He couldn't move forward in establishing a new relationship until the old ones were completely resolved. He knew God had given him Jamaica for a reason. Her spirit was thirsty for new life. He knew Patsy would present the possibility of a painful challenge. He braced himself for whatever that meant. He was not blind to the prospect of rejection, yet he was not afraid of its arrival.

He could thank his children for his rekindled confidence. They reminded him of his true essence. They helped him see what had been lost in the battle for survival. There was a good man in there waiting to come out again. He got lost somewhere between Durham, North Carolina and Dallas, Texas. He was back and ready to be used to do the work of the kingdom.

AUGUST

Unity in Diversity • Examination • Imperishability

There is something in every one of you that waits and listens for the
sound of the genuine in yourself. It is the only true guide you will ever
have. And if you cannot hear it, you will all of your life spend your
days on the ends of strings that somebody else pulls.
-Howard Thurman-

YEARS HAVE A WAY OF TEACHING important lessons. Lessons about
love and hate. Lessons about victory and despair. Lessons about
walking in purpose and suffering consequences. The years mold a
person. It's not the joy that makes one stand tall nor is it the pain
that destroys you; it's the delicate balance between light and darkness
that gives life purpose. Darkness is not the enemy. It is there to lead
the way to freedom.

Simon sat in meditation before the beginning of another day. The
years had been filled with suffering. He reflected on the teachings of
the Buddha. The Buddha teaches the primary cause of suffering is
the desire to escape it. Life as we know it leads to suffering in one
way of another. The cause of suffering is attachment to or craving
for worldly pleasures and clinging to life as we know it. The Buddha
teaches that we suffer due to the delusion that our happiness or
unhappiness is attached to things or people. Suffering ends when
the cravings end. Freedom comes when a person overcomes the
delusion that pleasure is found in things and other people. This is
when Enlightenment is achieved.

For years, Simon had preached this truth. He joked that the Buddha was a good Christian. The teaching of Buddhism gave him a structure for dealing with human suffering. He fought against the Christian pursuit to overcome suffering by filling their voids with things and people. The emphasis on external manifestations of pleasure and success kept them wrapped in a vicious cycle of frustration. Their desire for things kept them from being free.

Things and people got in the way of their faith. The more they achieved, the more they needed to overcome the pain they felt. It was never enough. The more they obtained, the more they needed to purchase. The conversation of faith was reduced to how to obtain the next blessing, the next thing to prove their standing in God's kingdom. Suffering followed their quest for things.

They needed more, and then more, and then even more. The more they came to worship, the more they needed to satisfy the delusion. This new purchase will make me happy, they prayed. This new home or the new car will finally put me over the top. They prayed and paid and fell further and further away from their freedom. Things controlled their spirits. The Buddha was right. The desire for things resulted in suffering.

People served the same purpose. The need to be loved controlled their peace. They moved about the walk of faith in need of a partner to push them over the top. A husband will get me there. A wife will bring joy. In their quest for finding that special person to make them whole, they found suffering with each frustrating moment. Each time that man proved to be a mistake. Each time that woman breaks his heart. Each time with energy invested in finding that perfect mate, suffering follows. The other person holds happiness in their hands. The key to pleasure is found in their willingness and ability to fill that empty space. It is a delusion. It all ends up with suffering.

Simon examined his path to discover the validity of the Buddha's claims in his own life. The years had groomed him to give up on his quest to end the suffering. He was moving toward Enlightenment with an ease that came after letting go of his desire for things. It came after admitting the grip of their delusion. They could not please him in the way he desired. He needed more than the temporary high of a new purchase or the afterglow of sex. Pleasure had eluded him due to his obsession with the wrong things.

The church could not please him. His Enlightenment helped him see the torture of church worship. His love for God was replaced with an admiration for the institution created to reflect God's truth. He fell in love with the energy of black faith, the sway of the music, the thrill of the sermonic moment, the release in each holy dance. He sought pleasure in the life of communal worship, and was reduced to suffering when the institution questioned his style of expression.

His cry for release from the work of black faith led him down the path of deliverance. He walked away from it all in hope he would find pleasure. It didn't work – his backslide – because in doing so he walked away from himself. He walked away from his passion and love for the people he served and the God who called him to be present within the suffering. He sought a release from suffering by getting away from the suffering. This delusion led him deeper into the suffering. By walking away he passed on his freedom. It was the easy move, not the faithful action. Faith called him to reject all claims of pleasure wrapped in human packages. The Church could not hand him pleasure.

He used the Church like cocaine – a quick high hoped to fix the pain followed by the despair of a letdown. The stuff provided the same intended outcome. His BMW 745i was purchased to bring attention to a successful life. It sat parked as one of the last reminders of what used to be – a life of more than enough. He gazed at his extensive watch collection: the Breitling Aerospace, Cartier Tank Francaise, his Pierre Kunz, and his favorite, the Roger Dubuis Golden Square. Each cost more than four thousand dollars. He nodded his head in disgust "What was I thinking?"

His suit collection was a who's who in men's fashion – Baroni, Gianni Manzoni, S. Cohen, Valentini, Tallia, Cesare Attolini – so much spent to draw attention to his desire to please. His flirtation with life among the rich and famous left him empty. Gone was the work at the big church and teaching at the university. Gone were the days of lavish trips around the world and expensive gifts to prove his worth. Simon was flirting with poverty now. From riches to rags in less than a year, and he kept smiling as he watched his fortune fade away.

The tears stopped coming in May. The red rocks of Sedona filled his vacant spirit with divine comfort. He found solace in the presence of his son. There, in Sedona, real meaning came back to him. More than the luxury car he drove and impressive wardrobe, more than the delusions of their comfort, he found his true purpose while watching the rising and setting of the sun over those red rocks. No longer would he play the role of the victim. His life was rich due to the gift of people. People like those at The Light House who loved him purely and supported his vision. People like Chris and Carmen, his wonderful children, who rose above the fray of poor adult decisions to make sound decisions.

He recognized the hindering of the women in his space. For too long they too served the role of the drug du jour. One day Jamaica filled his veins like heroin in the hands of a junky. The next day he inhaled Patsy's embrace like a crack head in search of a moment of release. Each woman became a delusion of peace. Each came to take away the suffering in his way. He needed them to feel better. He needed them to press on for another day.

Their rejection led to his suffering. With each phone call not answered. With each word of another man in the way of their love, he suffered more and more. He gave each power over his Enlightenment, power over his freedom to be whole. Now, he walked on higher ground. The sound of the angels followed his footsteps, and the beat of scared drums filled his ears with internal praise. God was carrying him beyond the pile of bills stacked high on his desk. Late notices and the threat of disconnected services glared as he passed the desk. They begged his discontentment. They mounted high in hope of robbing him of his peace. It didn't work.

He looked at his watch. It was 9:25 a.m. He popped a bagel in the toaster and grabbed cream cheese from the refrigerator. The phone rang as he pulled the bagel from the toaster.

"Simon, talk to me."

"Why you have to sound so sexy when you answer the phone," Jamaica laughed.

"It's my morning voice."

"You should keep it all day."

"I'll work on it. So," he paused to take a bite of the bagel. "How things been?"

"I have some good news. My attorney was able to negotiate a settlement with the station for $25,000 in a lump payment and one year of salary and benefits," Simon had prayed that Jamaica would get enough to take her time in deciding on what to do next.

"That's what I'm talking bout."

"There's more."

"What you got?"

"Part of the agreement is they can't communicate any of the stuff around why I left the station. If they do they have to pay me for another six months."

"Now, that's what I'm really talking about. Sounds like the door is open for you to move on."

"Got some more Simon," she sounded like a child at Christmas.

"Bring it on girl"

"My agent has a number of stations interested in me. Simon, the network wants to talk to me. NBC in New York viewed my tape and they want to talk to me about work."

"Sounds like this might pave the way for a blessing," Simon paused to take another bite. "Jamaica, you can't keep a woman like you down. You rise to the top."

"I'm so shocked by how all of this came together, Simon."

"You shouldn't be. Not many can stand up to what you do. All they have done is to set you up to walk into a better situation. You have a chance to make more than you ever imagined."

"I know, Simon, but that doesn't matter anymore. I need more than that now."

"What! Super Diva is changing her ways!"

"Shut up, Simon," they both laughed. "I'm just saying all of this has taught me a lesson. I have to make some changes. This could have ruined me."

"That's true. The good news is it didn't."

"I thank God for that," Simon smiled as he listened. "It was that grace you keep telling me about that pulled me out of this mess."

"True that. Sounds like you are growing on the inside. That's what it's all about," he took one last bite of the bagel. "So, what are your other options?"

"Oakland, Seattle, Philadelphia, Detroit, Chicago and Durham," Simon was shocked with the mention of Durham.

"Did you say Durham? As in the Bull City?"

"I did. I asked for that one."

"What's up with that?"

"You know. I'm looking for a change," she stopped before saying more. "Aren't you happy that it's a possibility?"

"I'm happy if you're doing it because it's best for you. If you are doing it just because of me it could be a mistake."

"I don't see how, Simon."

"If you come here thinking we're going to be a couple again then you might be hurt. I can't say if that will happen. I'm in a different place right now."

"I know that, Simon. We've had that talk."

"So, what's up with Durham?"

"I think I might like it there. It's not such a bad place."

"You know you like the fast life of the big city."

"Yeah, and the fast life is what got me in trouble. I liked the big city because I thought I could hide behind all those people. You know, everybody knows everybody in small towns like Durham. I got a rude awakening, Simon. If shit wants to find you it will. No matter where you are. It will find you. What you do in the dark will come to the light."

"Watch yourself," Simon laughed again. "Preacha' Man may be rubbing off on you."

"Is that such a bad thing? I like this new Simon. I was a fool not to get to know him before."

"That's not your fault, Jamaica. He wasn't around before."

"Well, nothing is firm yet. I'm just saying Durham is an option for me. At least I know that I have a friend there if I do decide to come. Know what I mean. It helps knowing somebody."

"I feel you, Jamaica. I feel you."

"I go to New York next week. Wish you could meet me there, Simon. No strings."

"Don't think Patsy would like that."

"You still with her?"

"Last time I checked."

"What's that supposed to mean?"

"Got a few problems we're working on. Only time will tell."

"So, there's still hope for your Diva?"

"Only God knows what tomorrow brings. As for today I'm with Patsy. Do you understand?"

"I do. You want to be faithful to the woman you say you're with. That's admirable."

"It's like this, Jamaica. I can't control what she does. I can't worry about what she is doing or who she may be doing it with. The only thing I can control is how I deal with my own life. I want to be accountable to God in all I do. Like I told you before, I'm tired of playing games with my life and looking for women to fill an emptiness that only God can fill. I'm sick of that. It's like women were a drug to me."

"Is that how you felt about me? Was I like fucking crack?"

"I'm not going to lie to you, Jamaica. What we had was good. Real good. It was the best I've ever had in a relationship. You opened my eyes to what love should be like. The only missing piece was in your inability to embrace my work. I was forced to decide and that shouldn't have been the case. I need a woman who can love all of me and understand why I do what I do in this work. That was the only part that was wrong before I found out about the other part."

"You still mad at me about that?"

"No, how can I be? I left you, Jamaica. You had every reason to go back to that son of a bitch."

"OOO, you sound jealous. I like that."

"A part of me is jealous. Another part is hurt. Another part is confused. A part is angry at myself for leaving you. All of that is true. At the end of the day none of that matters. All that matter for today is the air I breathe right now. I can't change any of that, and I can't allow your actions to rob me of the joy of my next breath."

"Have you stopped loving me?"

"Never. I won't let myself stop loving you. Why would I? You have a special place in my heart. Because of you I stand in this new place. I've grown because of our experiences together. I have no desire to lose that special feeling of loving you. There is no need to let it go or force myself to think it is no longer there."

"Do you desire making love to me, Simon?"

"Of course I do. What kind of question is that? I would love to hold you again. I'm tempted to go there, but I won't as long as I am in a relationship with another woman, or as long as I feel that being with you will only be physical. I need more than that now. It's not like before, Jamaica. I need to be with a woman who understands me and loves the real me."

"I'm trembling listening to you, Simon," her voice began to crack. "I don't know how to say this."

"Just say it."

"I really want to hear you preach."

Simon sat in the styling chair at Sincerely Yours Salon. Glenda twisted his locks as the customers shared views ranging from politics, the world of entertainment and love. They were in the middle of a heated discussion regarding infidelity. Simon did his best to bite his tongue as the women in the room shared their aggravation with the state of the world of dating.

"People just need to be honest with each other when they get into a relationship," Glenda said. "It don't make no sense to have to deal with a person cheating when you can let the other person know up front that's what you want to do. If you want to be with other people, be with other people, but give me the option of deciding if I want to deal with that before you go out."

"I know that's right," Monique, the other stylist at the salon added. "There's no need to get all upset if the person you're with isn't ready to make a commitment. Just let me know. I get pissed with all of the games."

"I want my man to be committed to me," Janice, one of the customers chimed in. "Ya'll can talk all you want about being able to deal with a man who has this woman over here and that one over there and you in the middle, but I ain't playing that. What is mine is mine."

"I understand that, but if he comes to you and says he's not ready to be committed you can't do nothing but respect that. I can deal with that if the understanding is we both are free to do whatever we want. The person should have that option. Just don't lie about things. Just tell the truth," Glenda added.

"Couldn't it be that people don't tell the truth because it's part of the game," Simon had remained silent as long as he could. "If you tell the truth up front doesn't that rob a person of the pleasure of seeing how much they can get away with?"

"You better talk on that some more, preacher," Glenda said.

"I'm just asking, couldn't it be that people aren't honest up front because they like living on the edge? They want to see how much they can get away with. They want to see how many men they can play at once. How many men they can trick into their web of deception. Maybe people aren't honest because they enjoy seeing how much they can trick people into believing."

"I get that but why is it that people think they have to trick people. Don't they know what goes around comes around?" Monique asked.

"People do it because they are insecure. Collecting people becomes a way of helping them feel better about themselves. The more they get, the better they feel. At least that's what they think. Problem is it doesn't work. It doesn't work because it takes so much to sustain that life of lies. They can't tell the truth because they are afraid that they will lose that person once they learn about what they are really doing."

"So, you saying cheaters cheat because they don't love themselves?" Glenda asked.

"They do it because they need the validation of that person in their life," Simon continued. "They need to be liked and loved. Once they put it out there that they aren't ready for commitment it exposes them for the person they really are – immature and unprepared for a real relationship."

"Why does a person have to be immature just because they're not ready to be with one person? Maybe monogamy is overrated in the first place and women are meant to be with more than one man," Glenda stated as she finished twisting a loc.

"The question then becomes what purpose does a person serve in another person's life? Are we in relationships just for sex, and find meaning in a variety of sexual relationships, or have we been created to be more than sexual beings? When we talk about being open to having relationships with more than one person, aren't we saying the reason for being with a person is limited to sex?" Simon asked.

"No, it could be that I can't get everything I need from one person," Glenda jumped in before Monique had a chance. "The one over here can pay my bills. This one over here can give me a great conversation and that one is fun to hang out with. Then I have one who makes love to me. What's wrong with that?"

"Nothing. All of those men are what you call friends. The one you have sex with is more than a friend. Now, if you are having sex with all of them then you are engaging in a deception."

"How's that?" Monique asked.

"Because of your formula. If brother A is for help paying the bills, brother B for conversation and C is for fun, then why are you having sex with those three when D is for that? If the other three serve those purposes with sex and the guy for sex is just for sex then you have three relationships that are a deception. You have formulated in your mind that they serve a given purpose, but you use them for something different."

"I see your point with that," Monique said. "But what if the one for sex does it better than the other three," the women in the room screamed. "Sometimes you need a maintenance man to take care of your business."

"I think that's fine if you want to limit your life to that," Simon laughed with the others. "I do believe there comes a point in life when you discover there is so much more to this thing than sex. Sex becomes a way of hiding from a real relationship."

"And what is a real relationship?" Glenda wanted to know.

"It's about having a person in your life to share your days with, to build meaning together and to hold hands when you get old. There comes a time when we need more than what we take for granted when we are horny," the women screamed again.

"I haven't been here in a long time," Bonita said as she examined a sculpture. "The last time was when we came together to view the Grant Hill collection of African American art with the Romare Bearden collection. That was amazing."

"Yeah, Bearden is one of my favorite artists," Simon commented as he viewed the work of Pedro Lash at the Nasher Museum of Art at Duke University. "I met this guy at a dinner party. He teaches art at Duke."

"His work is interesting," Bonita responded. "Where is he from?"

"He came to America from Mexico. He spent a lot of time in New York"

"I bet that was an interesting dinner."

"It was. I always love meeting people from different cultures. His work is really amazing. I had no clue that he is this good when we met."

"You know I miss hanging out with you," Bonita stopped to get his attention. "I always learn things when we go places."

"Not many people can appreciate work like Lash's. I like taking you to places like this because you get it. Most women perceive me as being an uppity Negro. I just love art," Simon smiled. "I have a love for masterpieces."

"The way you're looking at me I would think you're saying I'm a masterpiece."

"Bonita, that goes without saying" Simon started walking in an effort to change the subject. "Let's go check out the El Greco to Velazquez collection."

"Reverend Edwards! You better come back here and talk to me," her playful lashing caught his attention.

"What, woman?"

"Why you been avoiding me so much?"

"I'm with you now."

"Yeah, you are, but why now and not before now? What's going on with you?"

"I needed some company. That's all. And I do miss you, so I decided to hang out like old times. Okay?"

"Have you been running from me because of what I said at the coffee house?"

"No, I haven't been running because of that. I've just taken time to think some things through."

"Things like what?"

"Like what does it all mean? Like what do I do with all that it means? Like what is God saying to me?"

"Do you have any answers yet?"

"Some. I'm still praying about some of the others."

"I just wish you would let me know how you feel about us, Simon. That's all."

"The fact that we're here together should give you a clue. Don't you think?" he smiled. "Can we get back to the art Ms. 1,000 questions?"

"Just a few more, Sir."

"What? Jesus!"

"Yeah, you better call on the Lord," they giggled doing the best they could not to be too loud. "How are things between you and my cousin?"

"I suspect that you already know the answer to that," he gawked sensing she knew more than she was willing to say. "Things aren't what they could be, but that will take care of itself in time."

"Why do you take it, Simon?"

"Take what?"

"What she is doing to you."

"And what exactly is she doing to me, Bonita?" he stopped again. She detected by the change in his voice that there were things he did not know.

"You don't know, do you?"

"Know what?"

"It's not my place to say, Simon. Just be careful. That's all I can say."

"It's really funny," Simon chuckled. "Whenever I have a conversation about your cousin I'm told to be careful. It's obvious that people know something they don't want to tell me. Wow. This is some crazy shit."

"I know, Simon. I know. I'm just not the one to say. Not with the way I feel."

"I respect that. Truth is I know in my spirit that something's not right. I was born on a day but it wasn't yesterday. Bonita, this has nothing to do with Patsy. I'm cleansing for my own well-being. I do care for her and have prayed for things to work out, but I'm much more concerned with my own peace. I can't depend on her or any woman to make me happy. Things will come to the light for me, and when they do I will process it all and move accordingly."

"I get it. I think."

"I have to take care of that saga of the journey before I begin a new one," he smiled again. She smiled back. "Then I can be free to say those special words."

He grabbed her hand and started walking again. "So, can we move on with this gathering of friends?"

"Listen, Motherfucker, I need you to stop calling my woman," an angry voice called Simon. He was certain the caller had dialed the wrong number. "If you don't stop I will kick your black ass, you fake ass preacher."

He knew then it was not a wrong number. Something bad was happening. Something worse than he had expected. His heart pounded as he considered the assertions of the caller. "I don't know what you are talking about."

"You calling Patsy. Patsy is my woman. Stop calling her," the truth had come to light.

"Patsy is my woman. We have been dating for the past six months." Simon made his claim as the man in Patsy's life.

"Fuck that! She lives with me Motherfucker. Stop calling her phone. I see your number in her phone and I need for you to stop calling her." It all was making sense now. She was not calling because she couldn't.

"I'm sorry, man. I didn't know about you."

"Look, man. She told me you keep calling after she told you to stop. I need you to stop calling her. The last time I went to prison it was for kicking a Motherfucker's ass for some shit like this." Simon couldn't believe what he was hearing. Not only was Patsy cheating, she was living with the man. Not only was she living with him, he's a felon. Simon stood in shock. Anger came back. After months of living on the mountain, it came back. Rage filled his chest as it beat fast looking for a place to rest.

"Look man, back off with that. I don't need your threats. If it's like that between the two of you, take it. I don't fight over no woman. All I can say is I didn't know about you. If I had I would have backed off a long time ago."

"You telling me you didn't know shit about me?"

"That's right."

"All this time you been calling she didn't tell you to stop?"

"That's right."

"You two be fucking?"

"Ask her that question."

"I need to know if she giving you the pussy."

"I haven't seen Patsy in over three weeks."

"Did ya'll fuck then?"

"No."

"When the last time you fucked?"

"Ask her that question. All I can say is I didn't know about you. If you have anything to ask her, you ask her."

"You really didn't know about me."

"I didn't."

"That's fucked up, man. That's really fucked up. That bitch lied to me. Damn, man I might hurt somebody tonight. I ain't felt like this since I got out, man."

"It ain't worth all of that."

"Man, I was going to buy a house with her. I got this place because of her, man. Damn man. I was going to buy her that 745, man. She been looking at that car, man. I was going to get that shit for her," Simon listened to a man who loved his woman. Despite the hurt he carried, he felt bad for his being in the middle of fabrications. He felt bad that lies and deception caught him in the middle of his change, and that the hurt made him think about going back to that former place where violence evened the score.

"I'm sorry, man," he apologized for comments he made. "I've heard bad things about you man. You nothing like they said."

A rare connection was made by two men caught in the middle of a game played. Patsy's deception was exposed. The other boyfriend spent the night in jail for communicating threats to Patsy. Simon tried calling Patsy to see if she was okay. She never returned his calls. Like before, the calls went to voice mail, and he spent the night like before – long before – covered in pain and sorrow.

Enlightenment was lost for a moment. He had to press through the suffering. Pressing wasn't easy. It was like his last relapse after significant recovery. Getting back can be difficult after demons like these find your address. The locked door to his fragile side was opened again. He fought the whys and hows all night. He fought them the next day and the next. He retreated to that secret place where emptiness has no comrades and despondency has no friends.

This is what Saint John of the Cross meant when he penned the poem "Dark Night of the Soul." He wasn't surprised but it still ached. Rejection always does when it finds you in the middle of self-awareness. His isolation forced him to renew again, to seek a higher consciousness. The truth was under attack again. He fought going back to those old playgrounds welcoming him to enjoy blame games and pity parties. He fought, for days, the urge to give Patsy control over his victory.

It rained for two days. He sat on a park bench as the rain cleansed the emptiness away. He cried out to God and those sacred tears reminded him that God shared his pain. No, he was not alone. He rose from the wooden bench allowing the drops of rain to soak his face. "God, restore me! Take this pain away! Take it away!" the rain continued to fall as he stayed there drenched, his wet clothes feeling too heavy to walk in. He waited for the end of the rain. He waited for the end of divine tears mingled with his own.

It stopped. Finally, the tears stopped with the rain. He closed his eyes long enough for the sun to replace the clouds. It found its way around the dense formation that hid its always present glory. The sun appeared after the rain. He waited long enough for nature to speak. Long enough for God's answer painted in the sky.

He looked. It was there. A rainbow.

SEPTEMBER
Arrogance • Bravery • Wisdom

We must learn to regard people less in light of what they do or omit to do, and more in the light of what they suffer.
-Dietrich Bonhoeffer-

THE HARDEST PART WAS IN THINKING everyone knew. How many of his close associates knew about Pasty's deception? Why wasn't he told that she was engaged in a relationship with another man? Did the partners at the church know? Were they laughing at him for being a fool? It was obvious that something was wrong, yet he continued to be faithful. He continued to work hard to develop a meaningful relationship.

Simon fought the urge to go back. His rise to the top of the mountain felt too good to allow this setback to drive him back into the valley. The internal questions bothered him the most. He wanted to know what he had done to deserve this treatment. He wanted to ask if he was that bad of a man. He wanted to press past the obvious to get a better understanding as to why such lies had to be told to play games with his spirit.

He kept calling. She refused to pick up the phone. He wasn't angry; hurt, but not angry. Hurt because he had decided to remain in the relationship when all signs pointed in the direction of wrong doing. Hurt because of his pattern – staying with women who fail to return what he deserved, while walking away from women prepared to love him completely.

He wrestled over his choices. He seemed most comfortable with pain. The pain of a marriage long ended before it was lay to rest. The pain that came with incensed Church folks who hurled their venom any chance they got. The pain of a life falling apart – more and more each day – as he sought to do the right thing with no earnings to solidify his life. The pain of poverty was taking hold as the woman who made a promise betrayed his trust. She promised to stand by him, to be there to support him – no matter what. She promised to give herself to help take the pain away. She brought more pain than she healed. She took him back to that former place of delusion that he had worked so hard to overcome.

He prayed for the power of the principles to overtake him. He prayed for the comfort of God's Holy Spirit to land on him like innocent doves on the shoulders of the Messiah. He waited for that sacred voice to pave the way to greater healing. Healing beyond the words he spoke to trick others into believing all was well. He needed yet another resurrection. Death returned to force new change – again.

The life of faith is a series of deaths. Each death leads to new life beyond things feared. The fear of loneliness, or the glares of the masses, presses faith to travel new paths of discovery. Each death opens wounds unresolved under the shadow of the lies one speaks to oneself to make life less painful. Death removes the blanket of protection that veils the layers of wounds waiting to be shoveled away.

Death forces the telling of truth when there is no other place to hide. No place to pretend when the heart no longer beats in even pace. The rapid beat enthused by fear challenges that persistent gaze into the mirror. It is there where discovery begins. Not in the evil ways of those who harm the broken spirit, but in the movement of the self in allowing space for pain to grab hold of fear and to snatch life from those headed to spiritual discovery.

Death comes in the middle of victory. It's a reminder that life is not over yet, that there is more to conquer before the end of the celebration. Death comes on the ride up. Once close to the top. Close to finding rest and peace. It comes to shift the wheat of contentment.

There is no rest for those who travel that road less traveled. Simon's tears pressed through the questions. Through the why's and how's and when's and what's – his tears pressed him through all the pain. With each "Why me, Lord?" the silence was his answer. As always, the answer was found within.

It was 10:30 a.m. Already. Time had slipped by as he prayed his way through the best he could before making his way to church to preach to the people. Little time had been spent on preparation. There was no one in place to preach in his place. Service would start in 30 minutes. He moved the best he could to make his way to his car. After making it half way, he turned back. He had forgotten his Bible. No time to waste.

He prayed with each footstep. Please, step, Lord, step, help, step, me, step, make it, step, through, step, the day. He prayed as he wiped the tears and tried to calm the shaking of his body. He couldn't stop it, but he had to. The people needed him to preach to them. Ten more minutes before the start of worship. He sat in the parking lot to compose himself. "I'm ready now," he spoke those words more to convince himself. The Word had to be preached, in season and out of season.

The people walked in with smiles on their faces. They spoke. He didn't recognize their faces. It was all so cloudy. The tears dulled his vision. He smiled; at least he tried to smile. "You okay, Pastor," he heard the voice but did not see the face. "Pastor, you alright?"

He thought he said yes, but his body and spirit said no. No to the question. No to the challenge. No to wanting to be there. He moved forward in preparation, hoping to take his normal place. He stopped to pray. "Lord, Give me strength," merely a whisper. He needed strength to keep pressing. He found it there. Strength came. It came not from an unseen force. It came from the people – all of them – who came to place hands on the man they loved. Their pastor needed what they had received – the light of love. Simon needed their understanding and support.

He fell there, just inside the room where worship took place each week. He fell to his knees and cried openly before those who looked to him for strength. They understood his need. No judgment given.

No questions asked. They saw the man who helped them grow in need. They cried with him. They prayed with him. Countless hands and tears placed in his direction. The emphasis for ministry was Simon today.

"God help our Pastor," he heard someone pray. No faces came to mind. He felt the shame of his weakness, but they would not let him linger there too long. Some had waited for the chance to love him through the agony. They would not let him stop his release. 'Stay there, Pastor, let God heal you. We got you today. We know you hurting. We know you been through so much. Lord, bless our Pastor. God give him the strength. God show him we love him. God take care of this wonderful man."

He heard all the prayers. Then he stopped praying. Instead of pressing through he allowed them to pray for him. The community rescued him. Then it happened. Memories came back. God spoke through former days. He saw himself standing before the people at Shady Grove. He saw the looks on their faces. The disgust was obvious. They despised his ways and work. He saw it as The Light House prayed.

His pain shifted in that moment. While on his knees he felt what he needed – the love of the people. He felt the unconditional love of those who followed and believed in his work. "God, thank you for this family," his tears transitioned to symbols of praise. He received the comfort. He heard the voice he was waiting for, it was always there. It spoke through those with hands placed on his trembling body. The voice of God spoke to Simon through them.

"This is what you prayed for, Simon. This is what it means to be the Church. You are free to be loved by them. Be free and let the people minister to you. He rose from his brokenness to receive love from the people. Janice, Betty and Glenda, members of the liturgical dance ministry were the first to hug him. "I love you," each whispered as they embraced their pastor.

One by one they came. Each with the same simple message, "I love you…" He was humbled by the experience, but they refused to allow him to feel shame. They understood his burden. They had no need to know the details that caused his breakdown. They came to love and support him. In the middle of the line was Sophie. She came with a smile on her face. It was her chance to say what had been on her mind since the first day she came to The Light House.

"You know I love you," she held him tight. "You are such a blessing to all of us. Thank God that we have been given this chance to show you how much we love you. Thank God! Thank God!"

Her message defined the moment. The Light House was letting their light shine, and Simon needed their light. It was a moment of discovery. For Simon, it was a time of rediscovery. The call took on new meaning – once again. The once burdened place of human service became, in that moment of tears, his spiritual oasis.

Years of being placed on a lofty pedestal came to an end. The Light House took Simon down from the seat of unrealistic expectations. They set him free from being their source of inspiration. He stood with them, side by side, as one of the wounded healers. His strength was in his weakness and they embraced it as part of the human struggle. His pain became a part of the communal testimony.

Their journey was a shared story. Each tear became part of the village's story. They cried together – never alone. They cried together because each had cried through brokenness like this before. They could not judge Simon's tears after witnessing him live with the unreal expectation of producing a superhuman spirituality. They watched him whither as holy folks criticized every move he made and bashed him for failing to be like other ministers. Men and women called to lead cry too, and when they do, they often do it in the dark. When they do cry, alone in the dark, they rob the village of part of its witness.

God moves best when two or three or more are gathered together. It takes more than one fellow to be in the ship. The Spirit moves through the countless stories of transformation bound together by what makes them one. The tears bind them tight into a web wrapped in love. The need for more than what can be found on their own is what makes them authentic lights.

Simon's brokenness before the people helped pave the way for the liberation of the masses. His freedom set them free from the bondage of finding faith in those who lead. They could no longer seek perfection from him. He in return learned to trust them within that brokenness. His moment of weakness tempted him to fear their response to his pain. Instead, they saw strength in his pain. Those tears were too familiar for them not to reach out in hope of wiping them from his face. Simon learned to trust their response to his weakness.

Simon could now trust those he led with his human side. They knew his story – everyone knew. They knew of his divorce and the struggles with the leadership at Shady Grove. They imagined the pain of his struggles, but they never saw him as he endured an attempt to take the weight from his back. They imagined it all hurt, but in their minds they revered him for being different. He, they imagined, possessed some above human capacity to deal with such matters.

His tears told the truth they all knew yet refused to know. Simon was made of flesh and blood. He cried and worried and had a myriad of questions enclosed in a fragile mind. His tears before the people set him free to be human. His tears freed the people to embrace Simon as a member of the family of faithful in need of collective prayers.

"I'm sorry you had to go through that," Bonita had heard about Simon's conversation with Patsy's lover. "I hate that you had to learn about it like that."

"I'm not going to lie. It wasn't easy," Simon's Sunday morning experience made it easier to talk about. He still felt the ache of rejection, but a peace was coming over him. "Why didn't you just tell me, Bonita?"

"I wanted to," she paused to collect her words. "I wanted Patsy to tell you. I kept telling her that someone was going to get hurt if she didn't. I don't understand why she wouldn't tell you the truth."

"You know she won't talk to me," Simon had tried calling every day since it all happened. Two weeks had passed since his spiritual

Armageddon. The warring of his old and new visions of life forced a deeper reflection related to why it had happened.

"Why bother with her, Simon? Why don't you just leave it alone and move on?"

"I can't do that, Bonita," it was hard for him to understand himself. "I believe God wants me to be present with her through all of this. She did this for a reason that I can't understand, but I don't believe this defines her, Bonita. This is not Patsy."

"Maybe you are seeing the real Patsy for the first time."

"I know about her and Gerald," Simon Revisited the counseling sessions that led to Patsy's divorce. "I know about all of that stuff that happened between the two of them. I know they both had been unfaithful. I know her history, Bonita. I still don't believe this defines her."

"You still love her, don't you?"

"I do. If I didn't I wouldn't be hurting like I am. Part of my hurt is because I trusted her with my heart. I did something I vowed never to do. I dated a woman who is a member of the church I pastor. I saw that as a major ethical violation, but I did it anyway."

"Why her, Simon?"

"At first it was only physical attraction that led me to her. I was really lonely after the break up with Jamaica. I wasn't dating. I was tired of spending all of my time by myself. It all started because she was available and safe."

"So what changed?" Simon sensed the jealously in her voice.

"Things changed because I needed to believe that my loving her would change things. I tried to do things different this time, Bonita. I didn't allow my emotions to get in the way of my decisions. I knew something was wrong, but if what I felt was right I didn't want to be responsible for it not working this time."

"You can't blame yourself for all that happened, Simon. Don't you think you need to give yourself a break?"

"I cheated on Janet long before she started seeing Maurice."

"That's news to me," Bonita was shocked.

"It shouldn't be, Bonita. I cheated with you. Although we never crossed the sexual boundaries, I was making love to you every time we met. I was cheating because I had something special with you that I could not tell Janet about. Being friends is cool. There is nothing wrong with having a friend of the opposite sex, but when you have a friend that you have to hide that's cheating. You can't talk about it because you know; deep down, there is something wrong with what you are sharing."

"I didn't know you felt like that."

"The truth is I was being controlled by my fears. When I came back I feared my past would bring judgment on me. I walked on eggshells all over again while pretending to be free. I kept my relationship with Patsy on the down low out of fear of what people would say if they knew. I pushed her away because of that. I also pushed her away because of Jamaica. My love for Jamaica was too much for Patsy to deal with. She could tell my heart was still there, and she got tired of being in competition with her."

"I think you give her too much credit."

"I don't think so. I do believe she loved me. I believe she still does. I believe she did what she did out of pain. If I'm wrong it doesn't matter. What matters is how I function in all of this. I can't take it personal. Although part of this is about me, not all of it is about me. I can't be angry with her for what she did. What I can do is learn from it by looking at myself and growing from my mistakes."

"You telling me you taking all the blame for what she did?"

"No, I'm saying I have to learn from my mistakes."

"I get that, but why you need to talk to her?"

"That's the strange part of all of this. Even going through all of the pain, and I still am going through it, I can't help but think that I have a purpose in being in this place. All of it has taught me deep lessons about what it means to be a Christian."

"What kind of lessons?"

"I never really understood what it means to forgive, Bonita. With all those sermons I've preached about it, none of it really came home until now. I understand better what it means to love unconditionally. God is teaching me a lesson about the heart of God."

"She doesn't deserve your love, Simon."

"We don't deserve God's love. I think that's the point of it all for me. Everything that has happened to me over the past two years is helping me comprehend the faith I profess. All of those theology books fall short of giving me what I have received because of dealing with the ways other people's shit impacts my life," Simon was getting emotional.

"You have been through a lot."

"Yes, but it's all for my good, Bonita. It all teaches me a lesson about how I am to be more like Jesus. That's what I keep asking myself in all of this. What should my response be as a person of faith? I can't do things like I did in the past. I suppose that's what happens when you are stripped of the comforts you take for granted. It forces an inward look."

"Does that mean you would take her back?"

"I can't answer that. I don't know what will happen next."

"I don't understand."

"What don't you understand?"

"Simon, you have me sitting here waiting to stand with you in all you do. I love you because I know the real you, not the you people see. Patsy loved the former you. Don't you think that maybe she did what she did because she could not deal with the new you? I love the man you are today. I love the change in you. I see that change. I love you because I saw it as it unfolded and I loved what I saw coming. You have me waiting for you, yet you continue to be present for a woman who can't be what you need. I just don't understand that."

"I know it's hard to understand, Bonita. I don't get it myself, but I believe it's what God wants me to do."

Simon recognized the number on his caller id. After weeks of waiting and praying over what to say, she was calling.

"Hey Patsy," he was calm in his answer. He had left numerous messages requesting to have a conversation. He promised not to attack.

"I got all of your messages," she responded. "Thanks."

"How are you doing, Patsy? Are you okay? I need to know that you are alright."

"I'm doing better."

"You know I love you, don't you?" Simon asked.

"I don't know why after what I did to you," Patsy broke into uncontrolled tears. "I don't know why you want to talk to me."

"Because I know that you didn't do what you did to hurt me. I know that you love and care for me."

"I didn't mean to hurt you, Simon."

"I'm going to be okay, Patsy. You need to work on yourself. I'm not here to try to make you feel guilty about what happened. I really want to be sure that you are okay. We can't change what has happened. I do wish you had been honest with me so that I would have had the chance to walk away on my own."

"I didn't want you to walk away."

"Do you love him, Patsy?"

"I do. I have deep feelings for him."

"Do you love me?"

"You know I love you."

"Are you still with him?"

"I am. It's a bad situation. I should have never put myself in this situation. I have to fix it. I don't know how but I have to fix it."

"If he makes you happy you need to be with him, Patsy. It's that simple."

"I care for him but he's not good for me."

"Why would you say that?"

"He's still in the streets," Patsy paused as she processed what she was about to say. "I should have never got caught up with a man who just got out of prison. He's not ready to be what I need him to be."

"Patsy, sometimes it's hard because of how we fall for those who are no good for us."

"Like how you fell for me?"

"I wouldn't say that, Patsy. I'm not so sure you're not any good for me. I can see the real you beneath all that happened. There's a Patsy that didn't want this to happen. I think you did it because you were hurt. I have no bad feelings. I am hurt and confused but I'm not angry with you for doing this."

"I don't understand that," it all sounded too good to Patsy to be true. "You should hate me for this."

"You should hate me for what I have done. I loved Jamaica while I was working through my feelings for you. I held back my love and kept you a secret. It had to be hard for you to be with a man who couldn't celebrate our relationship freely. I allowed my fear of what people would think to come between the two of us, and I kept a space in my heart for Jamaica. I shouldn't have done that. It had to be hard for you to deal with all of that. You allowed another man to help you deal with the pain caused by my actions. I understand that because I have done the same thing in my life, Patsy. I can't be angry with you for doing what I have done myself. I can learn from my mistakes and grow, but I'm not going to waste time and energy making you feel worse when you feel bad enough already."

"I do feel bad, Simon."

"You need to work on your guilt and shame. This is not about us. This is about what you need to work through to get you back to the place you need to be spiritually. You haven't taken care of your spiritual side, Patsy. I'm not talking about going to church; I'm talking about letting God help you through all of this pain."

"Simon, I don't know where to start anymore. I feel so empty."

"All you can do is take one step at a time, Patsy."

"I can't even pray, Simon."

"Guilt will do that. It's hard to pray when you feel like God is angry with you."

"God is angry."

"The good news is that God loves us no matter what, Patsy. That's what grace is all about. It took me a long time to understand that. My hope is that this conversation will help you. I pray that your knowing that I'm okay will help you get past the guilt so you can get back on track with your spirit.

"Why you doing this, Simon?"

"Because I have to, Patsy. Trust me when I say this is God working in me. The old me would have walked away from you with no conversation or thought of continuing a friendship with you. I can't do that anymore because I'm in no position to judge you. I have to love you through this because God has loved me when I have rejected that love. I can't allow my lack of forgiveness to get in the way of your spiritual renewal. If I do that everything I preach is a lie."

"I'm sorry, Simon. I'm really sorry."

"And I've told you that I'm sorry too. Accept my forgiveness and start working on you. You need to take control of your life again. You need to look at how your decisions are impacting your spirit."

"I know, Simon. You're right."

"I'm not going to judge your man. That's not my issue with you. My concern is not that you were sleeping with both of us, but that you weren't being honest with us. What that says to me is that you haven't been honest with yourself. I support your decision to be with him. It is obvious that is what you want. You spend time with him. You have moved in with him. He has a place in your life that I don't. I'm not going to question that. I don't need to compete with him or dog him out to make myself feel better. I accept your relationship."

"I still need you, Simon."

"I'm here as your friend, Patsy. I can't walk away from you because God won't let me. I'm here to help you through this. You have to want to work through this. You have to ask yourself what is good for you. Is this a part of an old pattern that needs to be changed in your life. If you keep doing the same things over and over again you will get the same results, Patsy. It is important that you recognize that two men have been hurt because of your actions. There is a reason you need to understand that – so you change your ways. If you don't you will continue to make bad decisions."

"I know I need to change some things. I'm just so messed up right now."

"Yes you are. I'm not trying to preach to you, Patsy. I don't want to come off that way. I'm telling you all of this because I have been in your shoes."

"I know."

"I'm telling you to focus on you. Don't be afraid to call me if you need a friend. I'm on your side. I do love you, Patsy. I'm hurt. I want you to understand that you have hurt me deeply. I'm telling you that not to make you feel bad, but so you will understand that I cannot give you power over my emotions. If I do I give you what belongs to God. I have to free myself of your actions impacting my emotions. Do you get that, Patsy?"

"Kind of."

"I'm loving and supporting you because I need it for my own freedom. As hard as this is, I have to do it. I have to do it because if I don't I forfeit the blessing that comes with being able to love and forgive. That blessing is more important to me than holding on to all of that pain caused by what you or anyone else has done to me."

Anguish seems to always come in threes. It's the unholy trinity of life. Money problems, frustrated relationships, and work related issues – they team up to beat against the confidence of those seeking to find the Land of Promise. The ups of life are minimized by the downs that come in the form of a vicious attack of the unholy trinity. The assaults come unexpectedly. They come in the middle of relaxation from overcoming the last battle with one of the evil cousins. Simon was finding peace again. Peace from the terrible collision from a frustrated relationship. He rested too soon.

The caller ID said Herald-Sun. He was two days removed from his deadline. He picked up the phone assuming it was his editor. "Simon, this is Herman Bates," the managing editor had never called Simon. The change in ownership shifted his relationship with the power brokers at the paper. "How you been doing?"

"All is well with me, Herman," Simon, still dazed and not prepared for what followed.

"Simon, I just wanted to call to tell you we love your column. You serve an important role in this community."

"I'm glad to hear you feel that way," it sounded like a routine evaluation. "My work means a lot to me."

"We know that, Simon," there was a pregnant pause. "That's what makes this such a tough thing to do. You see, Simon, we want you to stay with the paper, but we can't afford to keep you at your current rate of pay. We would like for you to continue writing for us but we can only pay you $50 a week."

Simon was thrilled at the statement of confidence, but the cut was too much to consider. He couldn't say yes, not after working so hard to bring his pay up to a respectable amount. "I'm sorry, Herman. I can't do that. I just can't see taking that much of a cut."

"We thought you would say that," Simon sensed the disappointment. "Will you think about it for 24 hours and get back with us. Think about it and give us a counter offer."

"I'll do that," Simon already knew the answer. As much as he understood the paper's position he could not take a cut in pay. He wasn't willing to go backwards. Simon needed the money. Every little bit helped. He considered his voice in the community and all the hard work that had gone into building his reader base. He knew it was coming to an end. The last bit of stability he had was gone. It had been enough to keep him afloat – not much, but just enough to pay the bills and eat.

Simon reflected on Kierkegaard's *Fear and Trembling*. He remembered that Kierkegaard argued that faith is founded in the belief in the absurd. Faith is that which is contrary to reason. Faith for Abraham was illustrated in his belief that he would kill his only son to receive him again in his lifetime. He pulled the book from his shelf to meditate on the contrast between the "Knight of Faith" and the "knight of infinite resignation".

Both give up everything, but for different reasons, he processed. The "knight of infinite resignation" gives up all in return for the infinite. The sacrifice is made in view of what will be obtained after this life. The person who sacrifices continuously dwells with the pain of the thing lost. The "Knight of Faith" also sacrifices everything, but does so with faith that all that is lost will be given back. This trust is based on the "strength of the absurd".

Could it be that he possessed the type of faith that believed everything lost would be restored? He considered the possibility. He compared the thoughts of Kierkegaard against Buddhist propositions. He believed that the end of his suffering would come with the release of all delusions. As long as he clung to the thought that things and people would add something significant to his life he would suffer as a consequence of the loss of things desired. Kierkegaard was in conflict with Buddhist thoughts.

He wanted to hold to the notion that all things lost would be restored to him in this lifetime. He wanted to move forward with a faith that walked in the "strength of the absurd", but knew that as long as he did so he gave space for suffering to take control. Simon needed a way to deal with the decision before him. More than that, he needed a methodology to help him think through how to engage within his spiritual journey.

Should he move forward with a faith that believed everything would be restored in this lifetime, or release the delusion that things brought any measure of comfort? He prayed for an answer. He needed a way to merge these two powerful conceptions into a working spiritual process. As he grappled with the loss of his work at the newspaper, he meditated on the meaning of the other losses. The loss of love, money and work dominated his reflection.

This trinity of trouble had followed him for too long. Each held unique power over Simon's focus. It was time to put an end to their deception. Simon was determined to find a way to cast the enemies of his courage into the pits where they belonged. He sought answers in the old scholars of his faith. Wisdom was stacked against the walls in his loft, waiting to be regarded. Their covers spelled the names of their authors – Henri Nouwen, Dietrich Bonhoeffer, Jurgen Moltman, Anita Allen, Ruth Gilmore, bell hooks, Howard Thurman – men and women who had examined matters of faith. He looked to them to help him move past this new pain.

This was a time for remaking faith. All of his life came together in this deep moment of reflection. He moved past the emotions of the previous weeks. This time his mind went to work to think through the meaning of it all. From Nouwen's *Wounded Healer* to Bonhoeffer's *The Cost of Discipleship* From Moltman's *Crucified God* to Thurman's *Jesus and the Disinherited* – Simon searched for a way to live with his loss. He read about cheap grace and the vicious cycles of death and alienation. He read again Thurman's account of "the hounds of Hell".

Simon allowed his mind to work through his frustration. What will it be, Kierkegaard's absurd faith, or Buddha's end of delusion? He felt the energy of his mission. A joy overtook him in the middle of his search. Books lay stacked across the dinette table. A yellow pad with words scrambled in confusing order rested near the book he read in that moment. He stopped and smiled. He smiled and laughed.

"Thank you, Lord! I understand now. I do. I understand now!" tears came again. This time they marked the significance of his epiphany. It was both Kierkegaard and the principals of Buddha that would guide him. He had that absurd faith that his mind would be used by God to restore the work reflective of its potential. The work would not die; it would come again in his lifetime. He knew that to be true. It was Buddha's way in that he had released the need for things to define him. He was free of the control of their manipulation.

"I'm tired now," he laughed some more. The next day he called the Herald-Sun. Then he waited for God to restore the work that had been lost.

OCTOBER
Commitment • Reconciliation

The weak can never forgive. Forgiveness is the attribute of the strong.
-Mahatma Gandhi-

THE WORD IN THE STREETS was that Simon was no longer in Durham. Rumors have a way of catching hold. Once they do they flow like heaps of snow in an avalanche. The talk about Simon was the buzz of the city since his return to start his new age ministry. The people over at Shady Grove did their best to present Simon as a womanizing, gay, demon-possessed fool. None of it dazed Simon. He did his best to stay away from all that talk. He walked with tough skin protected by even thicker armor. His focus was on the people he served. Even more, he kept his mind centered on his spiritual development.

Rumors have a way of impacting the work of ministry. The partners at The Light House were under constant attack for following Simon. They were treated like a religious cult in need of intervention to release them from the hypnotic persuasion of Simon. "You still attend that church?" they were asked whenever a person brought up the subject. "I heard that he…" they would continue with a long list of the most recent gossip bait.

Simon's freedom became the source of confusion among Christians in need of a minister too scared to enjoy life to its fullest. His love for music and spoken word led him to places where people gathered to listen to artistic renderings. He would go to concerts. He went alone, first out of fear of being seen with a woman, but then because there was no one to take with him. Not yet. The clock was ticking on his breakthrough from all of the pain. He needed space to rekindle before opening up to another woman.

It wasn't time. Not yet. It wasn't time to ask Bonita out. Not time to Revisit being with Jamaica. Not time to consider giving Patsy another chance. It was time to breathe. Time to take a break from all of the disappointment and to find self-love void of the confusion that comes with working through pain with a woman in the way of introspection. Simon functioned in relationships in a way similar to how he supported those in the church. He offered more than love — he became the provider of spiritual insight and nurture.

After months of giving to others, Simon needed space away from the giving. Away from Jamaica's need for understanding and Patsy's need for forgiveness. He needed more than the burden of failing to fulfill Bonita's expectations. Simon craved room away from other people's pain. As much as he craved the touch of a woman, he wasn't prepared to give in to the demands of those he touched. He wanted to be sure — really sure — before opening his heart to the possibility of a connection.

Simon recognized that his work limited his ability to freely date. The issue wasn't his willingness to engage in that process. It was the expectations of the women who came in search of much more than a meal and conversation. Many were hoping for a commitment. He knew that his reputation as a womanizer could be further enhanced by going out, checking out, and then moving on after finding no compatibility. Simon made the personal sacrifice for the sake of his work.

It didn't feel like a sacrifice. He wore it freely. He found pleasure in spending time without a woman by his side. Simon cooked meals for one, took walks in parks, visits to museums and viewed movies to fill space. He laughed and danced with no woman there to share the moment. He sat alone as Joe Sample stroked the ivory keys at the Carolina Theatre. He enjoyed Stanley Clarke and George Duke's groove with no one next to him to celebrate that special moment.

It wasn't time. Not yet. This was a season of healing. After years of marriage, living with a woman and dating, it was his time to get to know this man he saw each day when he looked in the mirror. His journals were filled with new words. They lacked the back and forth ritual of sagas connected to women. The new words weren't about Jamaica and Patsy or Janet and her manipulation. These new words gushed across the pages like a new language. Like words spoken in tongues, Simon discovered a new vocabulary to define his life.

These were the words of freedom. New hope juxtaposed against the backdrop of a long journey found space on those pages. Simon wrote about loving life. He wrote about his special ways. He wrote about his love for music and art. He wrote about places he had been-Africa, Brazil, Russia, Paris-and how being there shaped his thirst for more.

No more words that reflected a passionate plea for deliverance from the entrapment caused by living in his skin. His analysis of the past took on new meaning. Freedom painted on the pages lifted him higher, and higher and even higher than before.

The rumors didn't stop him. They became the victuals of laughter. Food placed before him to laugh about. He was free. For the first time Simon stood above the fray. Above the thoughts of mean spirited people with evil intentions. Above the countless words intended to destroy his reputation and ministry. He walked in peace – for the first time –despite all they said. Despite the truth of his life, he walked in peace.

He took his once a week visit to the Imperial Barbershop for his shave and facial. Victor started cutting his hair when he first arrived in Durham. Simon continued to come after locking his hair. The barbershop provided him that rare place where black men could gather and tell their truth. It was the place to connect with those who share a common bond. The barbershop provided information, healing and hope. Simon came for more than a shave and facial. He came for rejuvenation.

"These pastors are robbing folks," Henry, one of the customers took center stage to rant and rave on the subject of the moment.

"Hush everybody," Victor joked. "Here comes a preacher." Simon walked in on a subject that would force him to share.

"Ya'll crucifying the preachers again?" Simon took his seat next to Victor's chair.

"We'd stop talking about it if the preachers would get their act together," Henry continued. "Don't make no sense what they do."

"That may be true in some cases, but let's not make all the preachers to be about the money," Simon was proud to share the other side of the issue. He knew the subject before being told.

"They all going to Hell," Henry lashed out proving he had an axe to grind that was personal.

"Not all," Simon interrupted. "I know I'm not in it for the money. I do this because I'm called to do it. There was a time when I fell into that group you talking about, but not anymore. The people of God made sure of that," some laughed. They knew the story.

"If you weren't kicked out you would be just like the rest," Albert, another customer chimed in.

"Well, I wasn't kicked out. I know that's what many people think. I walked away," Simon had to set the record straight. "But, that doesn't matter. In many ways I was forced out. I couldn't take it anymore. What you Church folks need to understand is how you set pastors up to be the way they are."

"It ain't our fault you pastors are lying, money hungry, cheating son of a bitches," Henry took a few steps closer to where Simon was sitting.

"No, my brother. Calm down. I didn't say it is your fault. I said we have sort of set things up to be this way," Simon didn't want to miss this chance to make a point that could help the men at the barbershop understand a little better what it means to walk in his shoes. "I'm saying people like to see their leaders function as superstars. You like to point at them as being one of the who's who of the city. You like talking about his or her wardrobe and new car. You like to brag about where you send them off to for vacation, and how much you raised for the pastor's anniversary. You like talking about where the children go to school. You like talking about how you take care of your man or woman of God."

"I don't like that," Henry lashed back.

"You don't," Simon took a deep breath. "Then why do you talk about the first lady when she walks in with her hair looking like a mess? Why you dog the good Rev. out when his suit is outdated, or he's driving around in a car on its last leg? Why are churches so into how that first family looks? Why are you so worried about how they make you look when they fail to represent you in the way you think they should?"

"They still a bunch of thieves," Henry kept coming at Simon.

"Just think of it this way," Simon shifted in his seat. "What happens when that pastor fails to look the way you think he should? What happens when he has hair like this and earrings like this? What happens when he dresses like this?" Simon pulls his hair, tugs his earlobe and pulls his collar to illustrate his point.

"Does he become the talk of the town when he no longer looks the way you think he should? Is the message any less because he fails to fit what you think he should look like?"

"He needs to respect the house of God," Henry shouts at Simon in disgust. "Some things should not be in the house of God."

"He needs to dress a certain way to respect God's house. Is that what you are saying?" Simon calmly asked, knowing that Henry was one of his critics.

"Damn straight!"

"So, are you willing to pay the cost for your pastor to maintain the lifestyle you want him to live by in order to respect God's house? Are you willing to give your pastor what is needed to do the job in a way that will not put him or her into debt to live according to your expectations?"

"They don't need all of that!" Henry came back.

"Depends on the church," Simon continued. "Some of your big name churches need all of that. They need you to make them look good. They define the worth of the pastor in relation to the way they look, where they live and what they drive. We place our ministers on these pedestals and then get mad at them for becoming what we want them to be."

"But this shit is out of control," another customer added to the conversation.

"Damn straight it is," Henry added his amen to the comment.

"I give you that. It is out of control. But, before you criticize those pastors ask yourself a question. Where are the people going to worship? Isn't it strange that we are drawn to the churches that promote the prosperity of its leader? Why are people drawn to those churches while staying away from others that are working hard to set them free from all of the crap that is out there? Why is that? Why do people want that?"

"I don't want that!" Henry came back.

"Maybe not. But so many people do. If you want to stop what the ministers are doing you have to get at why the people are coming to those churches. I think it's because they are lazy. It is easier for them to go to a church where the pastor makes faith easy. Bring me your money. Pay your tithes and offering. After you do that, plant a seed into this work. Just give us your money and God will open up the windows of heaven and bless you. People like hearing that because all they have to do is give."

"I hear you preacher. I hear you," Victor said while cutting a customer's hair.

"That's a lazy faith because it places all of the work into the hands of that pastor. God blessed our pastor, so if we bless our pastor and the work of the church we will get the same in return. In the meantime, faith is lost in all of that. What are you doing to get yourself in line spiritually?" If all you need to do is pay and pay, where is your responsibility in getting closer to God?"

"I feel you," another customer said.

"We get lost in the game called faith. My work is about shifting people away from deception. You have been robbed of things that connect you to a higher spiritual consciousness. You've been duped without knowing it. You try to pay your way to God. You look at a person's dress and you can't hear God because he's wearing jeans, has locs and earrings. You can't hear God speak because you're so tied with the way things look. Then you spend all of your energy discounting the worth of the message because of the way that person looks," Simon stood.

"Folks don't understand what is happening to their spirit. Too many are hooked on stupid. Why let the way a person looks impact what a person says? Help me out, John the Baptist. Didn't they discount you because of the way you looked? Help me out, Jeremiah. Didn't they cast you out of the temple because you told them they were worshiping a place rather than God? Help me out, Jesus. Didn't they crucify you for dogging them out for placing more emphasis on those long fancy robes than on the people they were called to serve?"

"That's different!" Henry came back.

"Is it? Oh, is it?" Simon was on fire now. "What is the difference? Didn't they back then worship their culture more than their God? Weren't they more concerned with how those Pharisees looked than with what the people needed? Aren't we more concerned with how our pastors look, our choirs sing, our church building look and how fine a reputation we have than we are about the needs of our community? Help me understand why we have so much crime taking place in the shadow of our churches. Help me understand why we have many people addicted to drugs and why folks won't come to the church for help. Help me understand why we have become so fashioned crazed that some can't walk into our churches without being starred at for failing to dress according to the fashion code."

"You just can't come to the church any way you want to!"

"So, let me get this straight," Simon paused. "You saying to me a person should stay away from their blessing if they don't have the clothes?"

"I'm saying people ought to respect the house of God."

"First and foremost my friend, God is present wherever we go. Not just that place we call the house of God. Last time I checked we are the temples of the Holy Spirit, but let me tell you a story."

"That's God's house and…"

"Like I said, let me tell you a story," Simon interrupted, denoting his disgust at the implications of what was being said. "Years ago when I was at Shady Grove, a woman came to the church to worship. She came off of the streets. She came just as she was, after a night of labor. She had just gotten off the late night shift. She came because she was tired of her job and wanted to make a change. She walked in filled with tears because her job was pulling her down and she needed to hear something to give her the courage to move on. She was a prostitute. She wanted to let it go, but she was not properly dressed. She came in with the wardrobe of her trade. She did not think about what she was wearing. She thought about the last blow job and how she wanted to make a change. The choir was singing that song "Jesus will work it out". She was in the right place," Simon remembered that day. It was a day that changed his life.

"I saw her crying from the pulpit. She walked in search of hope. The ushers met her before she could get in. They stopped her because her skirt was too short. Her blouse was exposing too much cleavage. Her scent was the stench of seduction. They would not let her in. They stopped her in her tracks. I watched as she cried. I came to her rescue. I walked from the pulpit to take hold of her hand. I felt her tremble. She told me she had to make a change. She told me she was sorry for not being dressed properly – that her mother had taught her better than this. She told me her story. It was time. She needed Jesus to forgive her of her sins and walk in new life."

There was silence in the room as Simon told the story. "I found a seat for her in the back of the church. Before granting her that seat, I prayed for her. It wasn't a sad prayer. It was one of thanksgiving. I thanked God for sending her to us to help lead her to the change she needed. She cried. I held her in my arms. People saw that embrace. They labeled it sin. Sin for embracing that woman who came looking like that. I told her God forgave her, that she could walk in her new life. She sat and listened and walked out after the service was over.

"Damn Rev," someone said. "That's deep. What happened?"

"I never saw her again. I suppose she couldn't face the people there. It doesn't matter. She received what she needed that day. I was rebuked for my actions. The deacons questioned what I did. It doesn't matter. God used me to do what needed to be done. Not my will, God's will be done."

"I hope she's alright," someone said.

"There's one more thing to be added to this story," Simon smiled. "I've been wearing jeans when I preach ever since that day."

"The interview with the network went well," Jamaica recapped her trip to New York as she got closer to finding a new job. "I think there's a good chance I'll get the job."

"That's wonderful. Is it top on your list of options," Simon contended Jamaica was positioned to pick her next job.

"I'm not sure, Simon. There was a time when I dreamed of working for the network, but just not sure I want to live in New York."

"You keep saying that," Simon was concerned that Jamaica would miss out on a great opportunity because of her fear. "I don't want you to miss out on a blessing because of what happened to you."

"What do you mean?"

"Sometimes we make decisions because of fear. You know, it's easier not taking the risk of the big opportunity because of fear of failure. It's easier not to try than to step into something only to discover you're not good enough for the work."

"I don't think that's it. I mean, I don't know what it is," Jamaica said, contemplating Simon's statement.

"You will admit that you have lost some confidence."

"No doubt."

"Why is that, babe?"

"I understand what happened to me, Simon. I fucked things up and deserved what happened to me. What hurt me is how they got rid of me. I know they had no choice, but it would have been nice if they fought harder for me. It didn't seem like they cared. Almost like they were happy it all happened to give them reason to let me go."

"That's just the way of the business, Jamaica."

"I know that, Simon, but that's what hit me. I was walking around like I'm the shit. I acted like I couldn't be replaced, like they needed me more than I needed them. At the end of the day I'm just another face among all the other pretty faces stacked in a file in the GM's office."

"You really feel that way?"

"Yeah, like I'm just a piece of meat. Once something changes everything shifts. It's the first time I understood what it must be like to be you," she paused to collect her thoughts. "You have to play by the rules of the game. No matter how much you bring to the table it doesn't matter if you don't play their way. They should have fought for me, but I wasn't important enough for them to do that. I'm not a person; I'm a person who moves their fucking numbers on the news so they can sell ads."

"So, what does that have to do with New York?"

"To be honest, Simon, I'm having problems with the industry. If I could I would walk away from it all. Like you did with that church. New York is so competitive. I love what I do because I love doing the news. Everything has changed, Simon. It's not about the craft. It's all about the image – the look, the sound of the voice, the persona. It's all so fake now. Then you have all of those damn crabs in the bottom of the heap waiting to pull your ass down so they can get your job. No matter how good you are there is always someone waiting in the wings to take your job."

"That's what you used to love about the business. You used to say that's what kept you motivated – knowing there is someone behind you looking to take your place," Simon responded.

"That was true when I thought talent mattered. It doesn't anymore. No matter how good you are, you will be replaced if they think you are a liability or if there is someone else who has something different. It's about what fashionable for that moment."

"So it's not just being afraid to fail?"

"That may be a part of it, but it's more about being tired of the politics of the business. New York would be a bigger version of what I got in Dallas. I miss the small town market. There I felt like I was a part of a family and there wasn't so much competition to stay on top. The thing that worries me is the thought that the industry has changed so much that maybe that's the mindset across the board. Maybe small market stations are the same way now because everybody is trying to get to that next level up. Someone in a smaller market wants in this market and someone in that market wants to get to that market. It's the big fish eating the small fish."

"Where does all of this leave you, Jamaica?"

"Confused about what to do next. I've given it a lot of thought. You know, stuff like what would I do if I'm not doing TV. Would I do PR? I don't know. The thing about it all is I love what I do. It's just the games you have to play to stay on the field.. I'm not sure how I would feel if I gave up on my life passion to be free from all the stress that comes with it all."

"I do understand, Jamaica."

"I know. It's so much like what you were going through while with me in Dallas. You enjoyed what you were doing, and we had a great time, but something was missing. That something was your call. You told me on that night that we all have calls. I didn't get it then, but being out of TV for these few months has forced me to think about why I do what I do. Do I do it for the check, or do I do it because it is my calling."

"I'm shocked to hear you use that word since you used to hate it so much."

"That's because I didn't understand it. I thought it meant like hearing a voice from God and seeing a burning bush. It's like you said, Simon, we all have passions. It's the stuff in us that won't go away. It's what we're good at. It's what brings you great joy and there is nothing that can make you feel in the way that doing that work does."

"So, you get it."

"I do get it. That's what makes all of this so hard. I've been living to do the work in the big market, but that really doesn't matter. What matters is not where I fulfill my passion but how I do it. I can be in the big market and only do half of what I'm good at. I may get paid big money to do that, and have big national exposure, but am I able to create work that satisfies who I am? The money can't replace my urge to be a good journalist."

"I see you have been thinking a lot, Jamaica."

"I have," she took a deep sigh. "And there's more."

"What else?"

"I've accepted that getting booted out of Dallas the way I did was a good thing. It forced me to face the truth about my work there.

You see, Simon, I wasn't doing what I'm good at. I was the face of the news, but I wasn't being a real journalist. The reason I went to J-School at Mizzou is because I wanted to uncover good stories. Stories like when I first met you."

"Oh, really now," Simon laughed as he remembered their first encounter.

"That was a crazy time. You were leading a protest on behalf of students demanding the hiring of black faculty and a freestanding black culture center. I wanted to dig into stories like that and make a difference. It's the reason I walked away from being a model, Simon. I had five, maybe ten good years left in me when I walked away. I left good money on the table to become a journalist and I did it for one reason."

"What was the reason?"

"I was tired of being viewed as nothing more than a pretty face who took good pictures. My pictures didn't talk. I wanted the world to know that I had more to me than a picture in a magazine. I wanted to investigate news and make a difference. I wanted to find and tell stories that no one else knew about. I wanted to tell the stories that weren't making it to the newsroom."

"And you feel you haven't done that."

"I've been reading the damn news. I sat on a desk and smiled and read. I'm not digging up stories anymore. I'm a TV model. I've gone back to what I used to be, and I want to do more than that. I'm not saying I don't want to be an anchor anymore. I want to have more input into building the stories that make it to the air."

"And you don't feel you can do that at the network."

"No, actually the network may be the place where I do that best. This may be my chance to get back into being a good journalist again."

"So, what's the problem?"

"It's all about the balance, Simon. You should know that better than anyone. You have to have the balance to make life more meaningful."

Simon placed the groceries in the trunk of his car. As he closed the trunk he heard someone call his name. "Pastor Edwards," he turned to see Larry Green approach him. He hadn't seen Larry since the night of the vote. He wasn't at church on that Sunday when he walked out the back to end his tenure at Shady Grove. Larry had stood on the side of those who voted to dismiss him.

"What's up, Larry?" Simon embraced his former church parishioner warmly. "Man, it's been a long time."

"Yeah, Pastor," Simon could tell that Larry was genuinely glad to see him. "Man, I've been wanting to see you since you got back. Where you having services?"

"We back at Northgate Mall. Back at where we started."

"I heard that you left town. People trying to find you, Pastor. Nobody knows where you at."

"We kind of hard to find. It's down in the basement."

"People miss you, Pastor. I miss you. Things ain't the same now that you gone from over there."

"I think it's probably for the better that all of this happened," they were more than mere words this time. Simon meant what he said. "I'm really in a good place. We're a small church, but I'm really happy."

"I heard that, Pastor. People miss your teaching. You know I ain't over there no more. I had to leave."

"I'm sorry to hear that, Larry. Shady Grove is a good church."

"Things are so different, Pastor. The teaching ain't the same. People miss your teaching."

"Thanks, Larry. I miss being there. I miss the people, especially all of the kids. That's the hard part of leaving a church. You're a family and it tears you apart when you have to leave members behind."

"Things just ain't the same, Pastor."

"They're not supposed to be the same, Larry. You can't expect the new Pastor to be me. I have my own style and gifts. He has his own style and gifts. The people over there need to learn to love and support him for what he brings, not for what they came to like about me. I'm not there anymore. I'm not there, in part, because they didn't want what I had to offer. Sorry to put it this way, Larry, but the people helped run me off from the church. Those same people who made it difficult for me to stay need to accept how they participated in that decision. Now, that's not a bad thing. I'm better off for it all, and they need to accept that they too are better off as well. You can't go back. You can only go forward."

"I hear you, Pastor, but the teaching just ain't the same. You always said something I could use in my everyday walk."

"Larry, different ministries offer different things. It could be that your spirit is in need of something different now. If that is true, you don't have to discount the work of one church as you look for what fits you. Things aren't supposed to be the same over there. They can't be because my personality and gifts are gone – for good. Accept that."

"That's good teaching, Pastor."

"I don't need to hear that Shady Grove is having problems, or that things aren't the same. That doesn't make me feel better. I pray for the church to thrive, Larry. I led that church for many years and helped build it up. It would hurt my heart to see it fall after investing all of that energy and prayer into the advancement of the work there. I'm going to ask that you pray for them. Don't spread bad news about the church. Don't go around talking about how things aren't the same now that Pastor Edwards is gone. You hear me, Larry?"

"I do, Pastor."

"There's one more thing that you and others must deal with."

"What's that, Pastor?"

"You have to face how you voted on the matter. I'm not angry for the way you voted. I don't need anyone's guilt or forgiveness. That night you stood on the opposite side. You voted based on your contention that I was no longer any good for the church. On that Sunday you didn't show up to sing with the choir. I can only assume you stayed away in protest. You had that right, Larry. You voted based on how you felt. I have no issue with that."

"You're right. I did vote against you that night."

"You voted your convictions. I would like to think you prayed before you voted. For some reason you felt you needed a different form of leadership. You felt so strong around your vote that you stayed away that Sunday. In your mind there was no reason for you to come back to Shady Grove. Not as long as I was there."

"You're right, Pastor. I'm sorry, but you're right."

"Larry, I don't need your apology. The pastor at Shady Grove does. They need it because of the way you just approached me. You are being flip-it in your approach to faith. Stand for something, Larry. Let me ask you a question, and be honest with me. Did God tell you to have this conversation with me?"

"No, I was just glad to see you."

"Then let me ask you another question, and, again, be honest with me. Did God tell you to vote against me?"

"No, I just did it."

"So what compelled you to vote against me? I'm asking you to answer the question not for me, but for your own peace of mind."

"You want me to be honest with you, Pastor?"

"I do. Again, not for me but for your own peace of mind."

"I did it because I was jealous of you," the confession was not what Simon expected to hear. He assumed Larry voted against him because he believed all the rumors. He assumed Larry thought he was gay and a womanizer. He assumed Larry wanted him out because of his liberal theology and push for a less formal worship service. "I was jealous because you so good at what you do and the women loved you so much."

"It wasn't God?"

"No."

"It wasn't because you felt I was no good for the church?"

"No. I didn't know it at the time, but I was jealous of you."

"So, how did you feel when you heard I had left the church?"

"I was hurt, Pastor. I didn't want to see you go."

"If you didn't want to see me go, why did you vote against me?"

"Because I knew it wouldn't work. It was so stupid Pastor. I voted that way because of my own issues and I've been feeling guilty ever since. Ever since I heard what happened that Sunday. I felt bad for everything I did, Pastor."

"Why do you feel so bad if all you did was vote when you knew it wouldn't work?"

"Because I spread lies about you. I was part of that group of people that put all of the foolish stuff out there. I wanted to believe that stuff was true because I was jealous of you. I didn't know it at the time. It was like the devil got hold of me and I couldn't let it go. It wasn't until later that I saw my true self. I was used to destroy a good man and I feel bad about it. Here I am dogging out Shady Grove and the man I dogged out is telling me I'm wrong for doing it."

"So why you stop going to Shady Grove, Larry?"

"Because I feel bad every time I step foot in that church. I can't help thinking about that night. Pastor, I gave the deacons $500 to pay Sophie. I feel like Judas when I walk in that church. I keep hearing the lies they told about you. I knew it was wrong but I was so jealous. Then it was like I was reaping some of what happened to you."

"What you mean, Larry?"

"I knew about your wife and Maurice. I was stupid enough to act like it was your fault. You know people said it was because you gay. I told people you're gay. I lied and told them a friend told me you gay. Your wife is with a stripper and people laughed at you behind your back like you ain't a man. They, no we, acted like you deserved to go through all of that."

"You know I didn't know, right."

"I found out the rest later. All that time people thought you knew about it all and that you were doing your own thing too. I just fed into all of that stuff. You know I was jealous because I wanted Sophie a long time ago. Before I got married I wanted her, but she wouldn't give me the time of day. She wanted you and it pissed me off. Then things got crazy in my life."

"How, Larry?"

"My wife left me for another man. She never forgave me for what I was doing to destroy you. She found out that I gave the deacons that money and we were never the same again. My wife loved you, Pastor. She still does. She would come to your church if she could find you. She talks about you all the time. She talks about how I helped run a good man off and how her life hasn't been the same ever since."

"I'm sorry to hear that, Larry. I know you love Judy."

"I do. I love her so much," tears started to come. "I lost her because of my jealousy, Pastor. My life has been destroyed because of how I got caught in the middle of a mess. The worst part is what I miss. I miss hearing you preach. I know I shouldn't bad mouth Shady Grove. You right bout that, Pastor. You really right, but it goes deeper than that for me. I got to tell you I'm sorry. You may not need it, but I do. I want my wife and children back, Pastor. I want my life back and I think God is saying to me that I need to make things right with you first."

"Larry, you have to let it go," Simon leaned against his car in preparation of the words that would follow. "My decision to leave was about me, Larry. It wasn't just about what happened in the church that night. It wasn't as much about Janet cheating. It had to do with me having to take some time to get free. I couldn't serve in the way I needed at that time. I was too broken to do it anymore. I needed time away, Larry. Time to get my act together. Do you understand?"

"I do, Pastor."

"During that week I went through an internal battle. It was like Isaac when he wrestled with God. I went through a weekend of a bunch of tears. Do you hear me, Larry?"

"I'm listening, Pastor."

"My whole life flashed before me. I remembered getting high. I remembered getting high for the first time. It was after getting word that my sister Crystal was dying from a brain tumor. I remembered being forced to suck a man's penis in the front seat of his truck. I remembered the pain I carried for all those years without knowing where it was coming from. I didn't understand it until the image of a penis in my face came to me."

"That's rough, Pastor."

"I remembered almost buying some crack over on Angier Avenue. It was after a church business meeting. I drove to the curve and this dude comes over to my car. He asked me if I was the police. The only thing I could think was I'm the preacher from around the corner that has been fighting to get you off the streets. I thought about stuff like that. I struggled with all of that. Things from my past that made me rethink if I wanted to do this thing anymore. I cried for two days, Larry. I couldn't get past all of that pain."

"I hear you, Pastor."

"There's more, Larry. There was this woman. Her name is Jamaica. I met her while in college. She is super fine. She came back into my life that week. In the middle of all that was happening she came back to me to tempt me. She offered me another way. A way with her. I felt guilty for feeling what I did. Then I discovered Janet was leaving me to be with Maurice. I discovered everyone else knew. Everyone was talking about my wife being with another man. I cried on the floor after leaving this fine woman. Are you hearing me, Larry?"

"I'm listening, Pastor. I hear you."

"What do you hear, Larry?"

"That you were hurting, Pastor. That you was carrying a lot of stuff."

"You're right. I was hurting. Not just because of what you did, or what other people at Shady Grove did. Not because of what Janet did, but because of all of it. I needed to believe in me again, Larry. I lost the passion to do this work. I had to leave it to find it. I was going through a change that I didn't understand, and now I get it. Now I understand my work for the kingdom. I understand it because of how I left it. I'm better for this journey, Larry."

"I can tell, Pastor. You seem to be so different. You are so real now. I can tell God has moved in your life."

"That's all that matters, Larry. Go tell Judy you saw me. Tell her what I said. Ask her if she still loves you. If she says yes, and I bet she will, tell her to come to church to see me. After that it's all in God's hands, Larry. It's all in God's hands."

NOVEMBER

Majesty of God • Patience • Return and Get It

*I can tell you that we have only one mission
and that is to make ourselves happy.
The only way we can be happy is by being who we are.*
-Don Miguel Ruiz-

SIMON TOOK A GOOD LOOK AT THE MAN looking at him in the mirror. It was hard for him to recognize his new self. So much had changed since his return to Durham. Nothing resembled what he assumed would be. The church was holding on with the 50 committed members it had, reminding all of the power in small numbers. Simon's finances had faded with each passing month without decent pay. There was no health and dental insurance to protect him from a potential setback. No retirement fund to add to his existing portfolio. There was only the week to week grind that ended with the gathering of faithful people. They kept him moving in faith.

He looked at the face of the man in the mirror. His long dreadlocks and earrings stood in grave contrast to the man who first stepped into the pulpit of Shady Grove. Gone was the clean-cut look that symbolized his endorsement of a more traditional faith. The tailor-made and designer suits were left hanging in his closet and blue jeans and designer shirts took their place. His look reflected an inner conversion. A change of mind related to his views of faith and life.

The shift in his wardrobe exposed Simon's internal grapple with the branding of his former life contrasted against the designer shirts of his new persona. He continued to flirt with the lure of the material world. It kept tugging at him, begging him to not let go completely. It was the cross he picked up daily-living in the world while trying, the best he could, not to be defined by the clothes used to cover his weakness.

Gone were the emotionally driven sermons packed with cute illustrations about what life would be like when he got to heaven. Gone were the special programs designed to highlight the work of the faithful few – the usher board, men's ministry, youth department. Gone was an emphasis on the workings within the sacred home of the faithful. Simon had changed. Loss had stirred a spiritual revival that shifted his life from a love for the outer to a search for his true identity.

"I missed you," Simon smiled at the man in the mirror. "I don't know where you have been, but I'm glad you showed up."

It was hard to imagine going back to his former self. His pursuit for wholeness led to a freedom that refused to go back to those former grounds of regret. This was a confusing place. His love for self emerged out of a willingness to love and forgive. Simon learned to trust for the first time. He trusted God to protect him. He trusted the Spirit at work within him. He walked liberated from the hindrances that come when you give people power to control your emotions. He refused to cry because of what they had done to him. No more tears for Jamaica, or Patsy or Janet or Shady Grove.

Simon was free to love and forgive void of pain and doubt. He took yet another deep breath as he prepared for another day filled with uncertainty. How would he pay his bills? Would there be enough to survive another week? He inhaled the Spirit and searched for peace within the confusion. Chaos would not win this battle.

He searched his closet to pick an outfit that spoke to his mood. "I must stop this flirtation with fashion," he laughed as he pulled Lucky Jeans and his Yoko Deaveraeux V-Neck shirt from the closet. He reached for the Merrell veer Slip-On shoes neatly placed in the section with his shoes. "People don't need to know you're suffering." He said as he took one last look at the man in the mirror.

The two wardrobes represented two phases of Simon's life: the one before his radical transformation. His life and love for fashion while at Shady Grove. The other was a statement about his life of change in his choices when the dreadlocks and earring came. It spoke to his love of fashion before leaving Durham and while he was in Texas. There was no money for new clothes. There was enough. "I hope I don't gain any weight, Dude," he joked with himself as he pulled the shirt over his head. "You still look good."

The lacks made it difficult for Simon to enjoy the things he loved. His love for music, fine food, art, travel and fashion were things he took for granted when the big checks piled up in his bank account. His spruced exterior hid the truth of his existence – he had more in common with the poor. His nice home and car hid the truth – he was living below the poverty level.

He moved within his freedom. Day after day, he smiled as if everything was well in his life. It was not a deception. His material existence did not define his view of life. Simon enjoyed the things others took for granted – the sound of birds chirping, the beauty of a sunrise, the cleansing power of the waters, the splendor of an infant's smile and the embrace of an old friend. Simon loved his life, and he refused to go back to that former place.

Simon struggled with the tension between work and freedom. His survival demanded something different. He needed a job to pay the bills. He needed benefits to protect him against sickness or injury. He needed savings for his future. Simon needed more than day to day existence; he needed enough to see past the end of the day.

Simon refused to go back to a place that forced him to fit into an alternative definition. Freedom felt too good to go back. As good as it felt, he knew the consequences of not having enough. Just enough was enough for him. Not enough was a different matter, but Simon kept smiling. He was free. He smiled even though doors continued to be closed in his face.

His reputation, experience and education scared people. He applied for work. He applied for jobs at Duke University, North Carolina Central University, city and county government, nonprofit organizations and with newspapers across the country. No interviews. No phone calls. No explanations. Rejection after rejection confused him, yet he refused to go back to that place of disappointment. He needed just enough to get by. A little more money to help get him through the days and months is all he needed. Simon prayed and waited for the right fit to come his way. Time was running out, and he worried that he would be forced to compromise for the sake of survival. He didn't want to go back.

He grabbed his laptop computer from the desk in his home office. He then stepped over to the bookcase nearest his desk and pulled Douglas Blackmon's book *Slavery by Another Name* and was headed down the steps to head out the door when the phone rang. Simon placed his laptop on the floor near the door and headed back to his office. He peaked at the caller ID before deciding if he wanted to answer. It was a strange number. The name Salem Baptist Church appeared.

"Simon Edwards," He expected to hear the voice of an old friend among the circle of celebrity clergy.

"Pastor Edwards, this is Deacon Robert Jacobs calling from the Salem Baptist Church in Brooklyn. How you doing, Pastor?

"All is well with me, Deacon Jacobs. Thanks for asking," Simon went through his mental record of churches he had preached for over the years. He had only preached in Brooklyn once. It wasn't the same church. He quickly processed the people he knew in Brooklyn.

"You probably wondering why I'm calling," Jacobs asked to put an end to the chit-chat.

"Actually, I was trying to figure out who I may know from your Church, Deacon. To be honest I can't think of ever being with you."

"You haven't, Pastor. We have never met."

"I'm glad to hear that, Deacon. I was beginning to think I was losing some of my memory," Jacobs laughed. The man had a sense of humor.

"No, we been checking you out from afar, Pastor. One of your former members at the Shady Grove Baptist Church is now a member at Salem. Jackie Thomas. She attended your church when she was in medical school over at Duke."

"Jackie!" Simon was happy to hear her name. "My God, I've wondered where she went. You tell her I said hello, Deacon. You have made my day," it was an emotional moment for Simon. Jackie was the first to embrace him after the failed attempt to cast him out at Shady Grove. He remembered her words to him when she hugged him. She told him he was free to do what was best now. If he were to walk away she understood, but she would always be thankful for what he had taught her. It was like Jackie knew what would happen next.

"Thought that might get you, Pastor," the deacon laughed. Jackie came up here shortly after you left Shady Grove. She got active in our church right off the bat. She kept talking about this pastor in Durham and how the people treated him wrong. She told us to never take our pastor for granted. She taught us how to love him."

"That sounds like Jackie, Deacon Jacobs. Sounds just like something she would say."

"Call me Robert, Pastor," he laughed again. "She told us you not much on titles and stuff like that. She told us you're a humble man."

"What she trying to do up there? Take me with her?"

"She did that alright. She did just that. God she has been good to us here."

"Wow, she really got busy."

"You can say that. She kind of stepped into things," Jacobs paused to shift the conversation. "There some things you may not have known about Jackie."

"We all have a story."

"That's true. You see, Pastor, when she was attending Shady Grove she was involved with our pastor. She fell in love with him while in medical school. When she finished her work down there she moved up here to marry him. She became our first lady. Isn't that something?"

"Jackie is the first lady! That's what I'm talking about."

"Seems like they had been dating for some time. Our pastor divorced his first wife a few years before they met. They fought letting the church know about it all. You know how that is, don't you, Pastor."

"You know I do."

"That woman stood before the church one Sunday and told her story. Wasn't a dry eye in the place, Pastor Edwards,"

"Call me Simon, Jacob."

"Got ya, Simon," they both laughed again. "That woman told her story. She talked about how she found God for the first time at Shady Grove. She talked about how you fed her Spirit. Then she talked about all the things they said about you. She talked about how much it hurt her because of how you fed her Spirit. She talked about the things going on behind your back and how she could tell how much you hurt when you stood before the people each week."

"She must have. The things she said to me. Wow. That was deep."

"She told us about the vote at the church, Simon. She told us everything that Sunday morning. Then it got interesting."

"What happened next? I got to hear this."

"That woman walked into the pulpit. Those old heads were about to go crazy."

"I bet they were."

"She told them not to worry. Don't worry because I'm not called to preach. I'm not coming up here to preach to you. I'm coming up here to stand by my man. I love this man. She took Pastor's hand, Simon. She looked him in the eyes and he lost it. That man lost it in front of all us. He was going through some things. We were treating him wrong. They wanted to get rid of him and he lost it when she said that."

"Wow," Simon felt those goose bumps all over his body.

"Wow is right, Simon! She then turned to the people as she held his hand. He was on his knees crying and she held his hand standing beside him. She told us she would not let us mistreat her man. She told us she had watched as the people hurt a good man down in Durham, but it wouldn't happen as long as she had a man like that in her life. She told us to stop the gossip. To stop the bitterness and to love him."

"What happened next?"

"She told us to come and pray for forgiveness. She told us to move past all of this. She called me up, Simon," the weeping on the other side of the phone was too much for Simon. He too started to cry. The story of a far away church became part of his testimony of change. "She called me up to pray for the church. You know why she called me up, Simon?"

"Why?"

"Because Pastor told her I was the only one he could trust. You know how that makes me feel, Simon? He trusted me."

"That has to feel good."

"It does. There's more."

"Keep going. Take your time."

"Jackie taught us to love our Pastor. When they got married it was a high time in the church. People who wanted Pastor out came completely around. That woman did all of that for us, Pastor. She helped us grow and we could see how her loving Pastor helped him grow. That man was never the same again," the weeping started again. "We gonna miss him."

"What do you mean? Did he get called to another church?"

"No, I wish that were the case," more weeping. "I wish that was true. He died last month, Simon. He was so young. He was only 42. Ate right, in good shape. No one expected it, Simon. He died while jogging. He was all by himself when someone found him out there on the side of the road."

"That's so sad. I'm so sorry to hear that. How is Jackie doing?"

"She's being Jackie, Simon. She keeps talking about how God blessed her to have him for those few years. Everyone at Salem feels so bad for her. We feel like we owe her so much. She is such a big part of who we are now. Can you feel what I'm saying, Simon?"

"I do. Man, I feel so bad for her."

"That's why I'm calling you, Simon. You see we had a group meet after church on Sunday. It was more than a group; it was just about the entire church. We came together to pray for her because she wasn't at church that day. It was the first time we hadn't seen her and we were concerned. One of the other deacons called her in the middle of service. She picked up the phone and she could tell Jackie had been crying. After getting off the phone she ran to the pulpit and told the church we had to meet at the end of church to pray for our sister. Everyone lost it, Simon. That woman has taught us so much."

"That's amazing."

"It is. The deacon who called her is a deacon because of how she told us we needed to have women deacons because Pastor Edwards said so," they both shouted in response. "Everything was always about what Pastor Edwards said. Our Pastor loved it. He was a big fan of yours, Simon. He would have the deacons listen to your sermons and discuss them. Before he died he wanted to have you come up here to celebrate the work we do. That man loved you too, Simon."

"Man. You have made my day."

"I'm not finished. See, we met at the end of church to talk about our sister. What came out of that was a decision of the church. We have decided, without ever meeting you, to offer to you to become our next pastor. I'm calling you today to call you to the church. It all makes sense, Simon. We already know you. We love you because you helped us get to this place. You nurtured our faith without knowing it, and we want to offer you the chance to come up here."

"I don't know what to say," Simon's heart was beating uncontrollably. Was this God's way of providing for his needs? "I don't know what to say."

"We know. It's a lot to absorb. We know. We told Jackie right after the meeting."

"What did she say?"

"She said her prayer was answered. She said it doesn't matter if you come. What matters is that we get it. The blessing for her is in what we did, not in your decision to come be our pastor."

"I don't know what to say other than I'm overwhelmed right now."

"There's only one thing to say."

"What's that?"

"Thank God for this day. Thank God for this day, Simon."

Simon knew not to look for a sign. If God intended to show the way it would come to him. It would come unexpectedly, and, more than likely, it would come in a curious way. Simon knew not to look for a burning bush or to listen for a thunderous voice. He waited and listened for his spirit to speak to his spirit. The answer was within, not from some extraordinary demonstration of divine order.

Simon had witnessed a myriad of examples of God's guidance. Countless conversations coupled with evidence of the worth of the work at The Light House kept him pressing forward. He moved expecting phenomenal things to happen. He was never disappointed. Simon was surrounded by limitless miracles. They were always there, even in the worse of days at Shady Grove, they were there reminding him of God's presence and power.

Miracles were happening in the shadows. There, where least expected, rebirth happened every day. Simon watched as the grip of brokenness was rendered hopeless in the presence of boundless hope. He watched as the Spirit strangled varied forms of addiction, robbing it of its power to evoke pain in the lives of so many. He watched as people broke free from the load of guilt and shame. He watched women wrecked after a series of bad relationships find the beauty of their true worth. He watched men end old habits and children change bad grades into academic scholarships. A flood of miracles surrounded Simon.

He understood his place in the process of the development of their faith. The light called him back to Durham to establish The Light House. Now, light glowed across the city. Ministry moved beyond the confines of a Sunday morning gathering. Ministry was incarnational, finding holy ground wherever and whenever one of the lights found a place to rest. Lights glowed in a variety of work settings, in classrooms, restaurants, and a variety of other places. Wherever they found themselves they took the light with them. They took the love and compassion of their faith with them after the last amen was spoken and the benediction was granted.

Simon saw it when they smiled. He recognized it when they left the church. They were not the same. His growth correlated with that of the people who witnessed his transformation. They knew something was different about the man who came out of hard days at Shady Grove to return to a city of disappointment. He taught them lessons about life and faith – not through his words, but by living those words and overcoming the endless hurdles tempting him to walk away.

Sophie was one of those miracles. She called to meet Simon. She said there was something on her mind, something she had to say. They met at The Blue Coffee Café for lunch. Her job at Mechanics and Farmers bank was close by.

"Hey, Gwen," Simon greeted the owner as he arrived at one of his favorite hangouts. "Looks like business is booming."

"Rev., you know I want what you got," Gwen joked as Simon ordered a coffee. "You ready to cook that Thanksgiving turkey, Gwen?"

"I was gonna come over to your place to eat since they say you the chef," they both laughed. It was the week before Thanksgiving. Chris and Carmen were flying in to celebrate with him.

"You know my kids will be here."

"We know, Rev. You told us three times," everyone behind the counter laughed.

"Can I come over?" Kim, one of the employees asked. "I heard your son is fine."

"Um, he is fine," one of the customers acknowledged. "I saw him play football last week. He is so fine."

"Hey, that's my boy," Simon played along. "Don't be messing with my baby."

"He ain't no baby," Kim said.

"Hey, Pastor," Sophie interrupted. Simon was having so much fun that he hadn't noticed her walk in. "They giving you a hard time about your fine son. You know he is fine."

"Oh no, there you go, too," he reached out to hug her.

"Well, at least we know where he got his looks from," Kim teased. "Daddy look good too." The place erupted in laughter.

"I ain't touching that," Simon came back.

"I wish you would," Kim toyed with Simon.

"What's up with you children? Dang," Simon bowed his head as if in prayer. "Sophie, let's get something to eat before these devils get a hold of me and make me have to pray for deliverance," he played along knowing it was just that – play.

They ordered lunch and took seats in the area away from the crowd. After a few minutes of talk related to Sunday's service, Sophie got to the reason for asking to meet.

"Pastor, I just wanted to meet with you to tell you how much you have changed," she began. "It's like you have become a new man."

"I hope that's a good thing,"

"It is a real good thing, Pastor. Not that things were so bad before, but this new you is really making a difference in the lives of the people who have watched you grow.'

"I appreciate that, Sophie. I really do."

"I had to say it because sometimes we fail to say what we feel," she went on. "You know that kind of got me in trouble in the past," she laughed it off knowing her past actions were over the top.

"We all learn from our mistakes."

"Yeah, Pastor. I have learned so much about the kind of person I am. In looking back I can't figure out why I thought you wanted to be with me. I was projecting my own feelings on to you."

"Sounds like you have grown too, Sophie."

"That's what happens when you get used and hurt a person you care about," she went on. "You know I never got the money they offered."

"Sophie, I never really got into if it was true or not. There was a lot of talk about your getting paid, but that wasn't an issue with me."

"I was supposed to get paid, but Deacon Andrews told me that since it didn't work I wasn't getting the money. He kept it all for himself and made it seem like I had received it."

"That's a shame."

"No, it's not," she smiled. "I see it as God's blessing. It has been easier for me to get over the guilt knowing I didn't get the money."

"That makes sense."

"When I came on that Sunday I was going to tell you that. I wanted you to know I didn't get the money. But then it hit me.

I didn't get it not because I didn't want it. I didn't get it because Deacon Andrews is a thief and a liar. I was still guilty because of my intent."

"The good news is you are forgiven, Sophie. There's no need to rehash any of this."

"Yes there is, Pastor. You see I don't know of anyone who would have forgiven me like that. My life has been changed because of it all. I had so much negative stuff inside me and I thought I needed a man to fix it. It wasn't a man I needed. I needed to learn to love me. I didn't think I was worthy of being loved until that day, Pastor. When everyone came up to me like that it was the first time I have ever felt love. I feel it all the time now. I feel it every Sunday."

"I can tell you are in a good place, Sophie. I'm so proud of you and the way you have turned things around."

"That's why I wanted to meet you, Pastor. I'm amazed that you are still with us. You have so many talents. Durham is too small for you. We all know that. We all know that you can go somewhere else and make the type of living you deserve. We know the sacrifice you make for us, and all of us are thankful for what you do."

"I know The Light House loves me, Sophie."

"We love you, but we haven't taken care of you in the way you deserve, Pastor. We need to take better care of you. That's why I wanted to meet with you."

"Thanks, Sophie. I really appreciate what you are saying."

"You see, Pastor," she collected her thoughts. "It's hard to explain this. It is really hard because I don't understand what is happening to me."

"Just say it."

"I don't want to sound like I'm crazy, but I keep having dreams about you. Not like the old ones when I let my desire for you to control my thoughts. This is different, Pastor. I keep having dreams that things are about to turn around. I've been having these dreams for about three weeks. I know it sounds crazy, but I see things turning around at the Light House and with you."

"Sounds like you have some faith working on your side. Praise God for that."

"I do, Pastor. I do have faith, but this is a strange feeling. When I meditate like you teach us it came to me that I should tell you about this dream. I don't know why, but I called you because I felt like I should tell you. It's more of a feeling than a dream. It's like I feel myself being a part of an unbelievable blessing. Does that make any sense, Pastor, or do you think I'm crazy?"

Simon felt a connection to her feeling. In the middle of her statement things changed. He felt a presence – a holy one – that made the conversation sacred. He wasn't looking for a sign. It came to him in a curious way. Simon knew God was speaking through Sophie.

Sophie's words followed Simon everywhere he went. "It's more of a feeling than a dream." It's what she didn't say that impacted him the most. Simon was weary of people who came with a message from God. He hated the prelude to their statement – "the Lord told me to tell you that…" He hated those words. He ran from the pretentious aura of their claims. It's what she didn't say that caught his attention. She didn't say God told her to tell him. She said she felt like she should tell him after she meditated. She said she didn't understand what it all meant. She didn't say God was going to do something, she said she felt like something was coming.

Her confusion moved him. Her confusion comforted him. She was the last person he thought would come to him with this feeling after all that had happened. Her entry into the work of the church was a miracle. The way she was moved to come, the way he was touched that day, the way the partners embraced her was all in the realm of the miraculous. Her words followed him for a reason. It was because of the phone call from Brooklyn.

The call that said "come be our pastor. We already know you. We love you here." That call. The one that could change his life and put him on the path of security again. That one. The one that would connect him to a work similar to the one in Durham. That call and Sophie's words followed him all day.

Despite the financial woes, his life in Durham was more than he ever hoped for. He had an inner circle of friends that made life interesting. He loved the variety of places he went, all with their unique group of people who brought an edge to his life. He loved the artsy side of the city and, most important of all, he loved the work of The Light House. The call forced him to think of whether it could be replaced with another community of believers.

Simon considered Jackie's statement to the members at Salem. What an amazing transformation. He reflected on what he would have felt if he had been the minister on the other end of her plea to the church. What would it have meant if Janet had done that? What if Jamaica or Patsy had made that bold move before the members at Shady Grove? What an amazing difference it would have made to have a woman like that by his side. Simon found himself, in the midst of his reflection, contemplating having that form of love in his life.

It brought him to his knees. He bowed against his sofa as Etta James sang "At Last" in the background. Simon had become content with being single. He found no need to stress during this season of discovery. He needed time away from the brutal cycle to find his true self for the first time. He found Simon Edwards to be a man of courage and strength. He found a man who had covered pain by filling his space with countless covers to protect his heart from disappointment. He covered aches with religion and women. Before it was women and drugs. He bowed and celebrated the growth of his inner spirit.

Sophie was right. A change had occurred. He labeled the change. It was there all along. The former reflection was an illusion. This man was the real Simon. All others were pretenders in pursuit of happiness. They robbed him of his identity and stirred the way to a path of constant frustration. Simon cried because this was the place. This was the place where he should have been all along.

Only one thing was missing now – a woman who understood the journey and loved him in his weakness. He wanted a woman by his side who could celebrate the place where he stood, not a woman who would manipulate him into going back to that former place. Simon desired a woman who could fight for the same causes, and love him, believe in him, and not rob him of his peace.

He wept not out of regret. It wasn't the lack that trigged these snuffles of joy. He poured elation to the divine out of gratitude. He thanked the divine for showing the way to the rest of the blessing that would be coming his way. He had not been prepared before for what would come his way. His own measures of worth and happiness deluded the gift that was to come. His eyes had shadowed the scene of God's design. But now, Simon was ready, for the first time, to be the man he needed to be with a woman.

Piece by piece, issue by issue, tainted purpose by tainted purpose, God remade Simon. Like clay in the hands of the potter, he was recast into this new man. After years of breaking his ego and forcing himself to see the blessing in the small things, Simon could see God. He saw God in the work. He saw God in the face of others. After years of being stripped of all excuses, Simon could walk free now. Free to work and love and be true to the man God had made him to be.

Transformation is hard work. It begins with an outer change. Hairstyles change. Other external alternations begin a shift in the way one thinks of life. The outward changes are easy. It's the inward work that hurts so much. It requires faith in the journey of change. It necessitates an understanding and appreciation for the need of change. It demands a willingness to fight for the right to change, even when others combat the claims of its significance. It moves when others back away, and it keeps moving when the change fails to manifest the things taken for granted.

Change requires trust. Trust requires faith. Simon had learned to trust the people at The Light House. His trust paved the way for pure faith. Faith is the negation of fear. It was the removal of all anxiety related to what the people of the church could do to him that freed him to explore and embrace his true self. He couldn't go back to being the man who pretended each Sunday. His was a faith that functioned in open space.

Gone were the lies told regarding his walk of faith. He no longer preached a message for the people that contradicted his own way of being. He was free to live and love void of the confusion that came with being the opposite of what he professed. Freedom demands accountability. Simon had grown to appreciate the tight bond between his actions and the way they impact the faith of those he loves. He could not use women for pleasure. As much as he desired their embrace, he could no longer take hold of them merely to satisfy his need for that moment.

Simon was free to grow within his faith. That freedom mandated a level of accountability greater than any he had ever known. It's what kept him from dating Bonita. It's what kept him from reaching out to find a woman to fill an empty space. Simon refrained from using the skills of his former life to fix what was hurting. His bones ached with the craving of sexual healing. Desire had not gone away. It was there even more than before. Months had passed since Patsy last touched him. He remembered the smell of her skin as he held her body against his own. He remembered her moans, the curve of her body and the sweet taste of her love.

He remembered the last time he made love. It left him wanting and waiting for more than before. More than a physical move of two bodies perfectly designed to meet. More than the best sex ever; he needed much more. He wanted a woman to stand with him with courage and defend his right to be. A woman willing to stand as he found the courage to be true to the man God made him to be.

His answer had come. Purpose had been found. Simon was walking within his purpose, and it could not be ruined by the love of a woman or the desire for things that took his focus away from the essence of its power. He was standing within it all along. He could not find it in another place. There wasn't more to be found to make the work more meaningful. The purpose was within him, living and working all along.

The call is to stand within it, not to run away to a bigger version of the call. Simon was called to embrace the life he was given, and, in the process of manifesting his faith, others would follow. The light at The Light House glowed because of this form of faith. It was faith absurd enough to believe that the sacrifice is worth what is lost.

Simon rose from kneeling covered in tears and glowing with peace. He reached for the phone to make the call. He wasn't moving to Brooklyn.

Simon walked in peace for the next two days. The members at Pilgrim weren't surprised that he wasn't coming. They agreed that the bond required the development of an ongoing relationship. Jackie organized a conference call with all the members present. Simon was at peace with his decision not to go. He was called to begin this work, and hardship would not run him away.

He went to the mailbox to pick up his mail. Two days had passed since he had been to the box. Simon didn't want the bills in the mailbox to rob him of the joy of his discovery. He laughed at himself knowing that running from the mailbox would not make those bills go away. He had to face them. A stack of junk mail covered one envelope at the bottom of the stack. It sat there waiting on the bottom – for two days. The envelope had the return sender name in its normal place. There in the left hand corner of the envelope was the blue and yellow logo of the business – Telepath.

Telepath. Telepath. Telepath. Simon remembered the name but couldn't remember from where. Telepath. Telepath. He tossed the load of junk mail in the recycle bin and headed to his loft. He held the light bill, phone bill and that mystery letter in his hand. Telepath. Telepath. He closed the door behind him, went to the refrigerator and grabbed the bottle of cranberry juice. Simon reached for a glass and poured the cranberry juice. Telepath. Telepath. He opened the letter. He screamed. He cried. He shouted. He cried uncontrollably. He wept with joy.

"Thank you Lord! Thank you Lord! Thank you Lord! Thank you Lord!" he couldn't stop crying. The prayers of the people had been answered. He thought about it. He had not checked mail for two days. It had been there waiting for him, that letter from Telepath, for two days. The same day he called Robert at Pilgrim. The same day he decided not to go to Brooklyn.

He held in his hand a check. He couldn't believe the number. $250,000. It came with a note: *Simon, when you get past your fears you can fly. Larry Green is my best friend. He's the one that brought me to Shady Grove back in the day. He shared with me the conversation you had with him in the parking lot. As I mentioned on the flight to Durham almost a year ago, I have been praying for a place to give. I know of no one more deserving than you. I will be in church with Larry and his wife soon. Your advice worked. They are reconciling. Again, fears can keep you from flying. Fly, my brother. Fly, my brother! Melvin Webb, CEO.*

DECEMBER

Hold fast to dreams, For if dreams die, Life is a broken-winged bird that cannot fly, Hold fast to dreams, For if dreams go, Life is a barren field, Frozen with snow.
-Langston Hughes-

"PASTOR, THEY'RE HERE!" Liz screamed as a bus pulled into the parking lot of the church. On the side was painted "Pilgrim Baptist Church". Simon ran to the lot to meet his new friends. They poured out of the bus one by one to meet the man who had touched their lives. Robert met him first with a big hug.

"We so glad to be with you, Pastor, I mean Simon, forget it, you my Pastor," they cried in each other's arms. They had talked every day since he called the church to say he wasn't coming. Simon embraced the man who had become a good friend.

"I'm so glad you could make it. It means so much to me," he unlocked from the tight hold to wipe his tears. The members of Pilgrim embraced the partners of The Light House. It was like a family reunion. "Where she at? Where my girl at?" Simon shouted as Jackie ran up to him and jumped in his arms.

"My Pastor!" everyone felt it. Everyone knew the story. They stood in the parking lot of the new home of The Light House. It was the first Sunday in the new building and the place was packed with people waiting to join in the celebration.

"Simon, do you mind if we talk to the two of you before you go in?" Jamaica smiled as she stood next to a cameraman. "We would like to do a follow up story."

"It's fine with me, Jamaica," Jackie said. "You and God had a lot to do with this day." Jamaica's story on the gift The Light House received after Simon was contacted by Pilgrim was the buzz of the city. People were so moved that they joined the ministry. Others gave more to support the work. Sophie was right about that feeling.

Jamaica was the Executive Producer and host of her own talk show. "From Jamaica" was a big hit in Durham. Her segment on The Light House was fed across the country. The Light House was glowing. Within 30 days the ministry was moved from just making it to fulfilling its vision. The partners were happy to be able to take care of Simon's needs. Simon was happy to be able to take care of the needs of those within the community. Sophie was right about that feeling.

"You know this means you're gonna have to marry me now," Jamaica whispered in Simon's ear. She was active in the ministry. Her life had changed. She too was happy.

Simon smiled knowing it was a real possibility. "Down girl. One day at a time. One day at a time."

He saw Bonita walking into the church. He followed behind and tapped her on the shoulder just before she reached for the door. "Hey, there," Simon said as he reached out to hug her. "I'm so glad you made it."

"I had to, Simon. This is an awesome thing. God just worked it out for you. I had to be here."

"You not mad at me?"

"How could I be mad at you, Simon? All I ever wanted was for you to be happy. It seems like everything you wanted is coming together," she said as she nodded in the direction of Jamaica.

"Only time will tell, Bonita. I'm not sure what will happen on the personal side of things. I know God has been moving through all of this, and I'm taking time to reflect and pray. You know what I mean?"

"I do, Simon. I do."

"I want you to know that you are a major part of my being here. You have been an amazing friend. I don't want to lose that friendship. No matter what, I need your friendship."

"You have that, Simon. You know that," Bonita walked away in preparation for church. Simon noticed Patsy staring at him as he opened the door for Bonita. She approached him with a look of disappointment.

"I guess I really messed things up," she said assuming too much from the embrace. "I have lost you."

"Just so you know, what just happened with Bonita was about our friendship," there was no need to explain, but Simon didn't want any negative drama to impede the day. "My focus is on getting through this day, Patsy. It's not about you, Jamaica, or Bonita. Today is about celebrating what God has done. I'm thankful for the women God has brought into my life. Each has taught me a much needed lesson. I'm taking it one day at a time."

"Is it over between the two of us, Simon?"

"If I were to answer that today I would say yes," he didn't want to answer. "I'd have to say yes because of where I am spiritually." Patsy walked away hurt by her own actions. Simon knew that she wasn't ready to deal with everything that comes with loving him.

Simon found Jamaica for a quick interview. Afterwards he kissed her on the cheek and told her he loved her. She smiled and walked beside him to find a seat. A change had come over her. "Simon," she called his name to get his attention. "I just want to say I'm sorry one more time."

"You don't have to do that, Jamaica."

"Yes I do. I'm sorry for not knowing how amazing you are. You are an amazing man. Simon, I thank God that you are called to this work," she smiled again. "You see, Simon, God used you to help me get to where I am today. Thank you for not giving up on me. Now go do what you do."

Simon walked into the sanctuary to take his place in the pulpit. It was his first time standing there.

He told everyone he didn't want to step into the pulpit until it was time to preach. He was ready now. The crowd rose in standing ovation as he walked in. The band played the theme music from "Shaft" as members of the choir sang "who's that man who can do his thang to make demons scream. Simon. Simon is a bad mother ... shut your mouth. We just talking bout Simon."

The roar of the crowd was the perfect introduction. Simon couldn't hold his tears. He was free to fly now. Surrounded by two loving congregations, he was ready to fly.

"I can fly now. I can fly," he cried out. Melvin came to his side as he allowed the tears to come.

"Fly my brother, fly. You're free to fly," there, in the presence of 600 people, Simon flew. He flew while embracing a white man who knew how to fly. He hugged the man who gave him wings to fly and he stood before those who gave him the courage to take that first step in flight."

He had run from his true self. A light brought him back. He slid back to his faith, and now he was free. Freedom is not what you run from. It is not what you run toward. Freedom is the courage to stand in your own skin and love what you feel.

Be free and fly.

THE JOURNEY

Those who helped along the way

It took me six years to write the sequel to *Preacha' Man*. The struggle was related, in part, to the need to give the story a chance to unfold. There is a close bond between the life of Simon Edwards and Carl W. Kenney II. So much so that many of the readers of the first book did their best to uncover the mystery of who is who, and what really happened during my days at the other church.

The twist and turns of my own life are reflected in the book more so in the thoughts of Simon versus the actual actions of the primary character. I needed time to work through my own issues caused by changes before completing *Backslide*. Thus, this book is a celebration of spirituality. These two works expose the myriad of concerns that make it complicated to be authentically human within the context of black faith. So much of what happens along the way strips men and women of God of their true selves. These works are written to help members of bodies of faith understand what happens when those who preach the Good News go home.

These books mirror my life in two ways. First, I have endured the heartaches associated with leading people who wanted my head on a silver platter. *Preacha' Man* was completed one month before I was ousted as pastor of the Orange Grove Missionary Baptist Church in Durham, NC. I saw the handwriting on the wall, yet lacked the faith to do what Simon does at the end of *Preacha' Man*. His departure was a celebration of liberation. Mine was an attack on my life and work that sent me down the path of rediscovery.

Secondly, I have grappled with loving while serving God's people. *Preacha' Man* was completed 30 days before my second divorce was finalized. Although the women in *Backslide* are the creation of my imagination, they represent many of the issues that come with being single in ministry. The conclusion is simple – the cloak of ministry does not protect men and women of faith from enduring what other folks go through. I do my best to force people to examine the man side of Simon while holding high the preacher side. Language is used to force readers to struggle with how to view Simon as a whole man rather than the creation of their own expectations.

With that being said, I must thank you, Connie Pope, for being the final chapter in the book not yet written. You have wiped away all my tears. You have removed all my fears. Hold my hand as we explore what it means to be one in mind, body and Spirit. To Mary Jones, for loving me as your own son and pouring hope in my spirit when I felt I couldn't take another step. Thanks to my three angels – Glenda Jones, Janice Webster and Betty Redwood – for loving and caring for me as I went through stuff that only you know about.

To my brothers for holding me up: Christopher "Play'" Martin and the late Bill Cherry for sharing in the vision. To the late Dr. Alan Nealy for fighting on my behalf while I studied at the Princeton Theological Seminary. Your death left a void. Dr. Jeremiah Wright, Dr. Johnnie Ray Youngblood, Rev. Harold Butler, Dr. Donald R. McNeal and Dr. Clanton Dawson for strong mentorship. To Dr. Robert C. Scott, Dr. Craig S. Keener, Dr. Howard John Wesley, Dr. Vanessa Abernathy-Enoch, Karen Thompson, Willetha Ar-Rahmaan and Richele James for being more than ministers under my leadership. To all the other sons and daughters in ministry- thanks for all you've done. Some made me stronger by loving me. Others made me stronger through betrayal.

To my parents Carl Sr. and Doris, for grooming me into who I am. Thanks, pops, for your take care of business approach to life. Your strength has made me strong, and you are my role model. Thanks, moms, for your kick them in the behind attitude. Your desire to make a difference has inspired me to do the same.

To the springs that sprang further than the spring sprang: King, Lenise and Krista Kenney, three amazing children. I can't believe you have grown to be so awesome! Can't forget Julian Kenney. It's okay to call me daddy. You're just like a son to me. To Sharonda and Andre, my niece and nephew, I can still bring you to your knees! Hey big sis, Sandra Kenney, love ya so much sugabugga.

And to all the partners of Compassion Ministries of Durham. To Victor, minister of music. You are more than a talented musician, you are a true friend. To Mama Lottie Hayes and Mama Thelma Waller for being faith for me when I couldn't see the way. To George Waller, Paul Megget, Joyce Ruffin and Bahari Harris for leading with integrity. To those faithful members of the praise team – Gerri Odum, Belinda Wiley, Kim Arrington, Kevin Harrell, Fred Holding and Alexis Moore for being there every week to sing us to the mountain.

Thanks to my team: Pandora Frazier (graphic artist-cover design), Dani Nation (editor), Amanda LaFrance (photographer), Katina Rankin and Angela Ray (public and media relations), Marlon Wilson (web consultation), Jeff Poe and Alicia Lange (webpage design), Kristal Burch (video production), Brett Chambers and Dante James (consultation) To my readers: Dianne Benze, Melanie Drane, Valerie Chestnut, Kenya Caldwell, Janice Webster, Florentine Neal, Charmaine Mickens, Michael Palmer, Candy Massey, Linda McCoy, Deborah Ann Debnam, Shelia Cross and Abosede` O. Copeland.

Can't forget my inspiration - Crystal Lynn Kenney - who died in 1976 at the age of 12. My baby sister continues to live within me. Love you girl!

Life is a celebration of community. These are some of the people who have nurtured me in faith. Thanks for all you do. We can fly now! We can fly!

-Carl W. Kenney II-